William Watson

Lyric Love

An Anthology

William Watson

Lyric Love
An Anthology

ISBN/EAN: 9783744768313

Printed in Europe, USA, Canada, Australia, Japan

Cover: Foto ©Andreas Hilbeck / pixelio.de

More available books at **www.hansebooks.com**

YRIC LOVE

AN ANTHOLOGY

EDITED BY

WILLIAM WATSON

AUTHOR OF 'WORDSWORTH'S GRAVE, AND OTHER POEMS'

London

MACMILLAN AND CO.

AND NEW YORK

1892

DEDICATION

TO

M. R. C.

FROM honeyed slopes of England's Helicon,
  Where'er the visits of the Muse beget
  Daisy or hyacinth or violet
Born of her tread, these floral spoils were won.
Some with caresses of the wooing sun
  Are passion-flushed and sultry-hearted yet ;
  And many with immortal tears are wet ;
And emptied of its odorous soul is none.

Take, then, this garland of melodious flowers.
  Till he, whose hand the fragrant chaplet wove,
    Another wreath from his own garden bring,
These captive blossoms of a hundred bowers
  Hold thou as hostages of Lyric Love,
    In pledge of all the songs he longs to sing.
                                        W. W.

PREFACE

IT will be readily apparent to readers of this volume that its aim has not been solely the collecting of the best love-lyrics scattered over English literature, but the bringing together, so far as was practicable under the conditions the Editor has imposed upon himself, of all the best English poetry having love as its personal inspiration or its objective theme. Thus, some of the old ballads have been admitted, where the prime agency was love, and where the literary result happened to be fine poetry. Thus, also, many passages have been selected from plays, and from narrative verse, where these could be detached from their context without disastrous impairment of their integrity ; the further condition being always observed, that although dramatic or narrative in form, they should be essentially lyrical in feeling. Obviously such a scheme offers a wide scope and range of selection, and upon a cursory view the reader may perhaps wonder that a larger harvest has not been garnered from three centuries of song, which brings me to the subject of the limitations I have thought fit to lay upon myself with regard to the principles of taste by which this selection has been guided.

In the first place, although I have taken, from six-

b

teenth and early seventeenth century verse, everything
that stood my doubtlessly fastidious as well as complex
tests of admissibility, it is none the less true that I have
drawn upon Elizabethan and Jacobean sources with a
sparingness which to some critical scholars, whose enthu-
siasm I respect on general grounds no less than I value
their erudition, will appear regrettable; but I have
decided upon this course after a careful exploration of
the field, and a conscientious effort to do neither more
nor less than strict justice to its poetic products. Among
the underwoods out of which rises the oak of Arden I
have indeed gathered many of the choicest of these
flowers of fancy, but I have not plucked them by handfuls,
much less harvested them by the scythe. With respect
to the Elizabethan lyrists, taken in the mass, a certain
amount of fanaticism has latterly been in vogue; and,
what is worse than fanaticism—for that implies the saving
grace of sincerity—a habit of conventional and factitious
admiration appears to be indulged in cases where knowledge may be supposed to invest its possessor with some
distinction and superiority. There are those who con-
stantly speak as though they would have us believe high
lyrical genius to have been of almost universal diffusion
in the days of Elizabeth and James; but as a matter of
fact most readers who have not the misfortune to be
specialists, and upon whom the necessity of professional
admiration is not incumbent, know quite well that with
a few splendid and memorable exceptions the song-writing
of that period was a more or less musical ringing of
changes upon roses and violets, darts and flames, coral
lips, ivory foreheads, snowy bosoms, and starry eyes.
The love-making seems about as real as that of Arcadian
shepherds and shepherdesses on porcelain. One may

lay it down as a general rule that—given the concurrent
quality of high poetic expression—the most truly interest-
ing effects in love poetry are where the shadow of two
living and credible personalities—those of the lover and
of his beloved,—are recognisably thrown across the
verse ; such is the case, for instance, with Shakespeare
and his dark lady ; but for the most part, in the amatory
song-writing and sonnet-making of the Elizabethan age,
there seems absolutely no personality at all either in the
singer or the sung ; it is an abstraction addressing an
abstraction, a shade apostrophising a shade.   The poet
seems to have a female lay-figure before him, and from all
one can gather, he might never have seen a real woman
in his life.   He carries hyperbole—a vice which only
great style can redeem — to intolerable lengths, and
demonstrates in every page how thin are the partitions
between extravagance and insipidity.   If he ever really
is in love, he is marvellously successful in keeping his
secret—even, one would suppose, from the lady.   His
goddess is a mere inventory of feminine graces, and she
might be constructed from a stock recipe of saccharine
ingredients.   She is usually, also, in the attitude of
obstinate resistance to a chronic siege, which adds
another element of monotony ; and truly, when we per-
ceive what a fantastic and absurd figure the beleaguering
party often makes, we scarcely wonder at the fortress
being so slow to capitulate.   In an age, too, when that
swan-song of chivalry, Spenser's *Faerie Queene*, was but
newly resonant upon the air, it is disconcerting to find
ever and anon a tone, a spirit, which to our modern
apprehension seems emphatically unchivalrous,—witness
the frequent phenomenon of a foiled *inamorato* crying
sour grapes when the hopelessness of his suit has at last

become manifest.   He turns upon the adamantine fair,
roundly tells her that henceforth he shall repay scorn
with scorn, and altogether behaves with a degree of in-
civility which the occasion does not seem to require.
Quite possibly it is a situation having more of an air of
reality than usually accompanies the literary love-making
of those spacious times ; but none the less there is a
painful want of knightliness about it.   To my thinking
even the fine and justly admired sonnet of Drayton's,

> Since there's no help, come let us kiss and part,

is not undisfigured in that way ; the line,

> Nay, I have done, you get no more of me,

being as coarse in feeling as it is rude in expression.
Taken as a whole, however, the poem in which it occurs
is so real, so convincingly alive, as to be worth a hundred
of the pranked and bedizened inanities of that period.

Whilst touching upon these matters one may note the
frequency with which an otherwise harmless exercise in
amatory verse is marred, for us moderns, by physiological
flowers of rhetoric which the mere caprices of time have
made archaic and grotesque.   In Shakespeare himself
the mention of the liver as the seat and residence of
amorous desire is far from being uncommon ; and when
Francis Beaumont writes,

> Did all the shafts in thy fair quiver
> Stick fast in my ambitious liver,
> Yet thy power would I adore, etc.,

we are apt to forget that our own employment of cardiac
symbolism is equally arbitrary, and may perhaps disqualify
some of the most admired love poetry of the present day
for inclusion in an English anthology published in the
year 2092.

In short, those enthusiasts to whom anything whatsoever bearing the name of Campion or Lodge or Barne-
field is sacred, and who seem to have difficulty in grasping
the idea that bad poetry could be written even in the
reigns of Elizabeth and James, must forgive me for
having acted, if not invariably, at least very nearly so,
upon the principle of disregarding the mere adventitious
distinction of antiquity.   Verse that is not intrinsically
of high value may often, of course, have a relative or
contingent importance, and a bearing upon the develop-
ment and evolution of poetry as a whole, which rightly
render it noteworthy in the student's eyes ; but in a book
like this, the absolute merits, not the historic or extrinsic
significance, of a thing are surely the only aspects of it
proper to be kept in view.   Not seldom, in regard to
old authors, Pope's observation is just, that

> It is the rust we value, not the gold ;

and, with respect to our indigenous literature, this tendency seems to me much more marked in our own time
than in Pope's, when the stricture could only have
applied to the pedantries of classical scholars.   Against
such a tendency I have deemed it best to guard ; and,
although this volume might very easily have been trebled ·
in bulk by the simple expedient of going to the Elizabethan Castaly with a draw-net, I have taken the more
troublesome course, often casting my line, patiently,
again and again,

> From morn to dewy eve, a summer's day,

to be rewarded at last with nothing more than a single
little golden-gleaming captive, or with none.   I have
some hope that the result has justified my procedure, for

I think there is in this book nothing that is not good poetry, and little that is not very fine poetry indeed.

Passing onward to the succeeding period, from the age which, with some latitude as to chronology, we broadly characterise as Elizabethan, I cannot but confess that to me there is something in the accent and air of the royalist or cavalier school of poets (and, saving Milton, Marvell, and Wither, all Parnassus was with the king) which, at its best, exceeds in sheer delectableness anything to be found elsewhere. Being neither in the decorative-pastoral spirit and florid Renaissance manner of the age that had closed, nor in the wholly mundane mood of the age that was to come, it caught something of the one by reminiscence, something of the other by foretaste, the result being an exquisite blend that will probably never be repeated. Whatever we may think of the lost cause in which Charles suffered, the sentiment of romantic personal loyalty which it evoked was certainly auspicious for the Muse. This picturesque and lofty figure, ennobled with the sombre grace of august calamity, aroused an emotion of service, and kindled a passion of allegiance, such as a pure Mary Stuart or a beautiful Elizabeth Tudor, hallowed with like misfortune, might have inspired ; and the effect upon the poetry of the time may be felt in a certain high Quixotic fantasy, and a kind of fine unreasonableness, which have yet a propriety and decorum of their own. With the passing of these poets the note of chivalric love ceased to sound, and during the whole of the long interval between Dryden's accession to the throne of literature and the romantic revival at the close of the last century, what is there in English love poetry to record ? There is, of course, Pope's elaborate study of a somewhat perilous

theme, and a wonderful piece of art it is, but too remote
from the sphere of ordinary sympathies; and there are
verses of Swift,—whom, of all writers, we associate least
with ideas of tenderness—verses addressed to Stella,
which are true poetry, and more than half belie their
writer's disclaimer of any feeling warmer than friendship
and esteem. The glow and nameless light are, however,
lacking to them, and the same may be said of his really
graceful verses "To Love"—

> In all I wish, how happy should I be,
> Thou grand Deluder, were it not for thee!
> So weak thou art, that fools thy power despise,
> And yet so strong, thou triumph'st o'er the wise.
> Thy traps are laid with such peculiar art,
> They catch the cautious, let the rash depart.
> Most nets are filled by want of thought and care,
> But too much thinking brings us to thy snare;
> Where, held by thee, in slavery we stay,
> And throw the pleasing part of life away.

These are not despisable verses, but much of what is
professedly dramatic writing is more really lyrical.

With regard to modern love poetry there is little that
needs to be said here. On the whole, one must admit
that "the freshness of the early world" has departed
from it; but, on the other hand, the fantastic insincerities
of our elder literature have departed too. The artificial
woe of the ancient amorist, whose days were a perpetual
honeyed despair and his nights one long lachrymose
vigil, is an extinct literary tradition; but a new, a
different, and, alas! a more real sadness has taken its
place—the modern world-sadness, the *Weltschmerz*,
which infects all we do and are, not excepting our
love-making—

> Ev'n in the very temple of Delight
> Veiled Melancholy hath her sovran shrine.

One suspects that the poet who wrote the unapproach-
able—

Hear, ye ladies, that despise,

or he who chronicled the card-playing of Cupid and
Campaspe for kisses, would have been somewhat per-
plexed, to say the least, with the "Sonnets from the
Portuguese," "The Unknown Eros," "The House of
Life," "Monna Innominata," "The Love Sonnets of
Proteus," and "Modern Love." Whether the rhythmic
speech of the latter-day lover has gained in depth what
it has lost in limpidness, who shall say? Concerning
which question the ensuing pages may perhaps afford
some material upon which to base a judgment.

I must not conclude these remarks without acknow-
ledging, with gratitude, the eminent courtesy which I
have received from the various living authors, who have
generously allowed me to enrich this volume with selec-
tions from their writings.

CONTENTS

CONTENTS

LOVE AND NATURE

CHIVALRIC LOVE

CONTENTS

THE WINGS OF EROS

LOVE WITH MANY LYRES

CONTENTS

LOVE'S TRAGEDIES

Sad and heavy was the love
That fell thir twa between.
Ballad of Clerk Saunders.

Joy, whose hand is ever at his lips,
Bidding adieu.

KEATS.

Thus piteously Love closed what he begat.
GEORGE MEREDITH.

AH me ! for aught that ever I could read,
Could ever hear by tale or history,
The course of true love never did run smooth ;
But either it was different in blood,
Or else misgraffèd in respect of years,
Or else it stood upon the choice of friends :
Or, if there were a sympathy in choice,
War, death, or sickness did lay siege to it,
Making it momentary as a sound,
Swift as a shadow, short as any dream ;
Brief as the lightning in the collied night,
That, in a spleen, unfolds both heaven and earth,
And ere a man hath power to say " Behold !"
The jaws of darkness do devour it up :
So quick bright things come to confusion.

WILLIAM SHAKESPEARE.

II

HELEN OF KIRCONNELL

I wish I were where Helen lies !
Night and day on me she cries ;
O that I were where Helen lies,
  On fair Kirconnell lea !

Curst be the heart that thought the thought,
And curst the hand that fired the shot,
When in my arms Burd Helen dropt,
   And died to succour me !

O think na ye my heart was sair,
When my love dropt down and spak' nae mair !
There did she swoon wi' meikle care,
   On fair Kirconnell lea.

As I went down the water side,
None but my foe to be my guide,
None but my foe to be my guide,
   On fair Kirconnell lea,

I lighted down, my sword did draw,
I hacked him in pieces sma',
I hacked him in pieces sma',
   For her sake that died for me.

O Helen fair, beyond compare ! ·
I'll make a garland of thy hair,
Shall bind my heart for evermair,
   Until the day I die.

O that I were where Helen lies !
Night and day on me she cries ;
Out of my bed she bids me rise,
   Says, " Haste, and come to me !"

O Helen fair ! O Helen chaste !
If I were with thee, I were blest,
Where thou lies low and takes thy rest,
   On fair Kirconnell lea.

I wish my grave were growing green,
A winding-sheet drawn ower my een,
And I in Helen's arms lying,
   On fair Kirconnell lea.

I wish I were where Helen lies !
Night and day on me she cries ;
And I am weary of the skies,
   For her sake that died for me.

UNKNOWN.

III

DEPARTURE

IT was not like your great and gracious ways !
Do you, that have nought other to lament,
Never, my Love, repent
Of how, that July afternoon,
You went,
With sudden, unintelligible phrase,
And frighten'd eye,
Upon your journey of so many days,
Without a single kiss, or a good-bye ?
I knew, indeed, that you were parting soon ;
And so we sate, within the low sun's rays,
You whispering to me, for your voice was weak,
Your harrowing praise.
Well, it was well,
To hear you such things speak,
And I could tell
What made your eyes a growing gloom of love,
As a warm South-wind sombres a March grove.
And it was like your great and gracious ways

To turn your talk on daily things, my Dear,
Lifting the luminous, pathetic lash
To let the laughter flash,
Whilst I drew near,
Because you spoke so low that I could scarcely hear.
But all at once to leave me at the last,
More at the wonder than the loss aghast,
With huddled, unintelligible phrase,
And frighten'd eye,
And go your journey of all days
With not one kiss, or a good-bye,
And the only loveless look the look with which you
    passed :
'Twas all unlike your great and gracious ways.

                      COVENTRY PATMORE.

IV

SONG OF QUEEN MARY

HAPLESS doom of woman happy in betrothing !
Beauty passes like a breath and love is lost in loathing :
Low, my lute ; speak low, my lute, but say the world is
    nothing—
           Low, lute, low !

Love will hover round the flowers when they first awaken ;
Love will fly the fallen leaf, and not be overtaken ;
Low, my lute ! oh low, my lute ! we fade and are for-
    saken—
           Low, dear lute, low !

                  ALFRED LORD TENNYSON.

V

FITZ-EUSTACE'S SONG

WHERE shall the lover rest,
  Whom the Fates sever
From his true maiden's breast,
  Parted for ever?
Where, through groves deep and high,
  Sounds the far billow,
Where early violets die
  Under the willow.

CHORUS.

Eleu loro, etc.   Soft shall be his pillow.

There, through the summer day,
  Cool streams are laving;
There, while the tempests sway,
  Scarce are boughs waving;
There, thy rest shalt thou take,
  Parted for ever,
Never again to wake,
  Never, O never.

CHORUS.

Eleu loro, etc.   Never, O never.

Where shall the traitor rest,
  He, the deceiver,
Who could win maiden's breast,
  Ruin, and leave her?
In the lost battle,
  Borne down by the flying,
Where mingles war's rattle
  With groans of the dying.

CHORUS.

Eleu loro, etc.   There shall he be lying.

Her wing shall the eagle flap
  O'er the false-hearted ;
His warm blood the wolf shall lap,
  Ere life be parted.
Shame and dishonour sit
  By his grave ever ;
Blessing shall hallow it,—
  Never, O never.

CHORUS.

Eleu loro, etc.   Never, O never.

SIR WALTER SCOTT.

VI

LOVE'S SECRET

NEVER seek to tell thy love,
  Love that never told can be ;
For the gentle wind doth move
  Silently, invisibly.

I told my love, I told my love,
  I told her all my heart,
Trembling, cold, in ghastly fears.
  Ah ! she did depart.

Soon after she was gone from me,
  A traveller came by,
Silently, invisibly :
  He took her with a sigh.

WILLIAM BLAKE.

VII

WHEN WE TWO PARTED

WHEN we two parted
  In silence and tears,
Half broken-hearted
  To sever for years,
Pale grew thy cheek and cold,
  Colder thy kiss ;
Truly that hour foretold
  Sorrow to this.

The dew of the morning
  Sunk chill on my brow—
It felt like the warning
  Of what I feel now.
Thy vows are all broken,
  And light is thy fame ;
I hear thy name spoken,
  And share in its shame.

They name thee before me,
  A knell to mine ear ;
A shudder comes o'er me—
  Why wert thou so dear ?
They knew not I knew thee,
  Who knew thee too well :
Long, long shall I rue thee,
  Too deeply to tell.

In secret we met—
  In silence I grieve,
That thy heart could forget,
  Thy spirit deceive.

If I should meet thee
  After long years,
How should I greet thee?—
  With silence and tears.

GEORGE LORD BYRON.

VIII

TRIOLET

WHEN first we met we did not guess
That Love would prove so hard a master;
Of more than common friendliness
When first we met we did not guess.
Who could foretell this sore distress,
This irretrievable disaster
When first we met?—We did not guess
That Love would prove so hard a master.

ROBERT BRIDGES.

IX

THE BANKS O' DOON

YE banks and braes o' bonnie Doon,
  How can ye bloom sae fresh and fair!
How can ye chant, ye little birds,
  And I sae weary fu' o' care!
Thou'lt break my heart, thou warbling bird,
  That wantons through the flowering thorn;
Thou minds me o' departed joys,
  Departed—never to return.

Aft hae I roved by bonnie Doon,
    To see the rose and woodbine twine ;
And ilka bird sang o' its luve,
    And fondly sae did I o' mine.
Wi' lightsome heart I pu'd a rose,
    Fu' sweet upon its thorny tree ;
And my fause luver staw my rose,
    But, ah ! he left the thorn wi' me.
                    ROBERT BURNS.

X

DIRGE FOR WOLFRAM

IF thou wilt ease thine heart
Of love and all its smart,
    Then sleep, dear, sleep ;
And not a sorrow
  Hang any tear on your eyelashes ;
    Lie still and deep,
  Sad soul, until the sea-wave washes
The rim o' the sun to-morrow,
    In eastern sky.

But wilt thou cure thine heart
Of love and all its smart,
    Then die, dear, die ;
'Tis deeper, sweeter,
  Than on a rose bank to lie dreaming
    With folded eye ;
  And then alone, amid the beaming
Of love's stars, thou'lt meet her
    In eastern sky.
           THOMAS LOVELL BEDDOES.

XI

THE MAID OF NEIDPATH

O LOVERS' eyes are sharp to see,
    And lovers' ears in hearing;
And love, in life's extremity,
    Can lend an hour of cheering.
Disease had been in Mary's bower,
    And slow decay from mourning,
Though now she sits on Neidpath's tower,
    To watch her love's returning.

All sunk and dim her eyes so bright,
    Her form decayed by pining,
Till through her wasted hand, at night,
    You saw the taper shining;
By fits, a sultry hectic hue
    Across her cheek was flying;
By fits, so ashy pale she grew,
    Her maidens thought her dying.

Yet keenest powers, to see and hear,
    Seemed in her frame residing;
Before the watch-dog prick'd his ear,
    She heard her lover's riding;
Ere scarce a distant form was kenn'd,
    She knew, and waved to greet him;
And o'er the battlement did bend,
    As on the wing to meet him.

He came—he passed—an heedless gaze,
    As o'er some stranger glancing;
Her welcome, spoke in faltering phrase,
    Lost in his courser's prancing—

The castle arch, whose hollow tone
  Returns each whisper spoken,
Could scarcely catch the feeble moan
  Which told her heart was broken.
SIR WALTER SCOTT.

XII

AIRLY BEACON

AIRLY BEACON, Airly Beacon,
  Oh the pleasant sight to see
Shires and towns from Airly Beacon,
  While my love climbed up to me!

Airly Beacon, Airly Beacon,
  Oh the happy hours we lay
Deep in fern on Airly Beacon
  Courting through the summer's day!

Airly Beacon, Airly Beacon,
  Oh the weary haunt for me,
All alone on Airly Beacon,
  With his baby on my knee!
CHARLES KINGSLEY.

XIII

(ELOISA TO ABELARD)

THOU know'st how guiltless first I met thy flame,
When Love approach'd me under Friendship's name;
My fancy form'd thee of angelic kind,
Some emanation of th' all-beauteous Mind.

Those smiling eyes, attempering every ray,
Shone sweetly lambent with celestial day.
Guiltless I gazed ; Heav'n listen'd while you sung ;
And truths divine came mended from that tongue.
From lips like those what precept fail'd to move ?
Too soon they taught me 'twas no sin to love :
Back through the paths of pleasing sense I ran,
Nor wish'd an angel whom I loved a man.
Dim and remote the joys of saints I see,
Nor envy them that heaven I lose for thee.

ALEXANDER POPE.

XIV

BRIGHT star, would I were steadfast as thou art—
    Not in lone splendour hung aloft the night
And watching, with eternal lids apart,
    Like nature's patient, sleepless Eremite,
The moving waters at their priestlike task
    Of pure ablution round earth's human shores,
Or gazing on the new soft-fallen mask
    Of snow upon the mountains and the moors—
No—yet still steadfast, still unchangeable,
    Pillowed upon my fair love's ripening breast,
To feel for ever its soft fall and swell,
    Awake for ever in a sweet unrest,
Still, still to hear her tender-taken breath,
Half passionless—and so swoon on to death.

JOHN KEATS.

XV

DAFT JEAN

DAFT JEAN,
The waesome wean,
She cam' by the cottage, she cam' by the ha',
The laird's ha' o' Wutherstanelaw,
The cottar's cot by the birken shaw ;
An' aye she gret,
To ilk ane she met,
For the trumpet had blawn an' her lad was awa'.

" Black, black," sang she,
" Black, black my weeds shall be,
My love has widowed me !
Black, black ! " sang she.

Daft Jean, the waesome wean,
She cam' by the cottage, she cam' by the ha',
The laird's ha' o' Wutherstanelaw,
The cottar's cot by the birken shaw ;
Nae mair she creepit,
Nae mair she weepit,
She stept 'mang the lasses the queen o' them a'.
The queen o' them a',
The queen o' them a',
She stept 'mang the lasses the queen o' them a',
For the fight it was fought i' the fiel' far awa',
An' claymore in han' for his love an' his lan',
The lad she lo'ed best he was foremost to fa'.

" White, white," sang she,
" White, white my weeds shall be,

I am no widow," sang she,
" White, white, my weeds shall be,
White, white ! " sang she.

Daft Jean,
The waesome wean,
She gaed na' to cottage, she gaed na' to ha',
But forth she creepit,
While a' the house weepit,
Into the snaw i' the eerie night-fa'.

At morn we found her,
The lammies stood round her,
The snaw was her pillow, her sheet was the snaw ;
Pale she was lying,
Singing and dying,
A' for the laddie who fell far awa'.

" White, white," sang she,
" My love has married me,
White, white my weeds shall be,
White, white my wedding shall be,
White, white ! " sang she.

SYDNEY DOBELL.

XVI

EDITH AND HAROLD

I KNOW it will not ease the smart ;
  I know it will increase the pain ;
'Tis torture to a wounded heart ;
  Yet, oh ! to see him once again.

Tho' other lips be pressed to his,
   And other arms about him twine,
And tho' another reign in bliss
   In that true heart that once was mine ;

Yet, oh ! I cry it in my grief,
   I cry it blindly in my pain,
I know it will not bring relief,
   Yet oh ! to see him once again.
                 ARTHUR GREY BUTLER.

XVII

TO EDWARD WILLIAMS

THE serpent is shut out from paradise.
   The wounded deer must seek the herb no more
      In which its heart-cure lies :
   The widowed dove must cease to haunt a bower
Like that from which its mate with feignèd sighs
      Fled in the April hour.
   I too must seldom seek again
Near happy friends a mitigated pain.

Of hatred I am proud,—with scorn content ;
   Indifference, that once hurt me, now is grown
      Itself indifferent.
   But, not to speak of love, pity alone
Can break a spirit already more than bent.
      The miserable one
   Turns the mind's poison into food,·
Its medicine is tears,—its evil good.

Therefore, if now I see you seldomer,
  Dear friends, dear *friend*! know that I only fly
    Your looks, because they stir
    Griefs that should sleep, and hopes that cannot die :
The very comfort that they minister
    I scarce can bear, yet I,
    So deeply is the arrow gone,
Should quickly perish if it were withdrawn.

When I return to my cold home, you ask
  Why I am not as I have ever been.
    You spoil me for the task
Of acting a forced part in life's dull scene,—
Of wearing on my brow the idle mask
    Of author, great or mean,
    In the world's carnival.   I sought
Peace thus, and but in you I found it not.

Full half an hour, to-day, I tried my lot
  With various flowers, and every one still said,
    "She loves me—loves me not."
And if this meant a vision long since fled—
If it meant fortune, fame, or peace of thought—
    If it meant,—but I dread
    To speak what you may know too well :
Still there was truth in the sad oracle.

The crane o'er seas and forests seeks her home ;
  No bird so wild but has its quiet nest,
    Where it no more would roam ;
  The sleepless billows on the ocean's breast
Break like a bursting heart, and die in foam,
    And thus at length find rest.
    Doubtless there is a place of peace
Where *my* weak heart and all its throbs will cease.

I asked her, yesterday, if she believed
  That I had resolution.   One who *had*
    Would ne'er have thus relieved
His heart with words,—but what his judgment bade
Would do, and leave the scorner unrelieved.
    These verses are too sad
  To send to you, but that I know,
Happy yourself, you feel another's woe.
                    PERCY BYSSHE SHELLEY.

XVIII

GODFRID TO OLIVE

(FROM *The Human Tragedy*)

ACCEPT it, Olive?   Surely, yes ;
  This ring of emeralds, diamonds too :
As I would take,—no need to press,—
  A leaf, a crown from you !
No rudest art, no brightest ore,
Could make its value less or more.

Gone is my strength.   'Twere useless quite
  To tell you that it is not hard
To have one's paradise in sight,
  Withal, to be debarred.
And yet the generous glimpse you gave
Was more than once I dared to crave.

Hard ! very hard, sweet ! but ordained.
  We know 'tis God's own world, at worst.
And we have only partly drained,
  And so still partly thirst ;
While others parched remain, or seize
Fiercely the cup and drain the lees.

So let us strive to deem it well,
  However now we stand aghast.
Earth, Heaven, not being parallel,
  Perforce must meet at last.
And, in that disembodied clime,
A clasp more close may not be crime.

You loved me too well to deny :
  I loved you far too well to ask.
Only a kiss, a gaze, a sigh,
  A tear,—and then a mask.
We spared the fruit of Good-and-Ill ;
We dwell within our Eden still.

O sunshine in profoundest gloom,
  To know that on the earth there dwells,
Somewhere, unseen, one woman whom
  No noblest thought excels ;
And that by valour to resign,
I make her more than ever mine.

Too late, too late, I learn how sweet
  'Twould be to reach a noble aim,
And then fling fondly at your feet
  The fulness of my fame.
Now—now,—I scarce know which is best,
To strive, or lay me down and rest.

O winter in the sunless land !
  O narrowed day ! O darker night !
O loss of all that let me stand
  A giant in the fight !
I dwindle : for I see, and sigh,
A mated bird is more than I.

God bless you, Olive !   Even so
  God bless your husband !   He, if true
To his sweet trust, to me will grow
  Only less dear than you.
But should he hurt his tender charge—
Why, hate is hot where love is large.

Yes—yes !—God bless your wedded lot !
  My beautiful !—no—no—not mine !
I scarce know what is, what is not,
  Only that I am thine ;—
Thine, thine, come aught, come all amiss.
No time, no fate, can alter *this* !
ALFRED AUSTIN.

XIX

REMEMBER me—on ! pass not thou my grave
  Without one thought whose relics there recline :
The only pang my bosom dare not brave
  Must be to find forgetfulness in thine.

My fondest—faintest—latest accents hear—
  Grief for the dead not Virtue can reprove ;
Then give me all I ever ask'd—a tear,
  The first—last—sole reward of so much love !
GEORGE LORD BYRON.

XX

TO ——

WHEN passion's trance is overpast,
If tenderness and truth could last
Or live, whilst all wild feelings keep
Some mortal slumber, dark and deep,
I should not weep, I should not weep !

It were enough to feel, to see,
Thy soft eyes gazing tenderly,
And dream the rest—and burn and be
The secret food of fires unseen,
Couldst thou but be as thou hast been.

After the slumber of the year
The woodland violets reappear,
All things revive in field or grove,
And sky and sea, but two, which move,
And form all others, life and love.

PERCY BYSSHE SHELLEY.

XXI

A CONQUEST

I FOUND him openly wearing her token;
I knew that her troth could never be broken;
I laid my hand on the hilt of my sword,
He did the same, and he spoke no word;
He faced me with his villainy;
He laughed, and said, "She gave it me."
We searched for seconds, they soon were found;
They measured our swords; they measured the ground:
They held to the deadly work too fast;
They thought to gain our place at last.
We fought in the sheen of a wintry wood,
The fair white snow was red with his blood;
But his was the victory, for, as he died,
He swore by the rood that he had not lied.

WALTER HERRIES POLLOCK.

XXII

TO JULIET

FAREWELL, then.   It is finished.   I forego
With this all right in you, even that of tears.
If I have spoken hardly, it will show
How much I loved you.   With you disappears
A glory, a romance of early years.
What you may be henceforth I will not know.
The phantom of your presence on my fears
Is impotent at length for weal or woe.
Your past, your present, all alike must fade
In a new land of dreams where love is not.
Then kiss me and farewell.   The choice is made,
And we shall live to see the past forgot,
If not forgiven.   See, I came to curse,
Yet stay to bless.   I know not which is worse.

WILFRID SCAWEN BLUNT.

XXIII

WALY, WALY

O WALY, waly, up the bank,
   O waly, waly, doun the brae,
And waly, waly, yon burn-side,
   Where I and my love were wont to gae !
I lean'd my back unto an aik,
   I thocht it was a trusty tree,
But first it bowed and syne it brak',—
   Sae my true love did lichtlie me.

O waly, waly, but love be bonnie,
 A little time while it is new !
But when it's auld it waxeth cauld,
 And fadeth away like the morning dew.
O wherefore should I busk my heid,
 O wherefore should I kame my hair ?
For my true love has me forsook,
 And says he'll never lo'e me mair.

Noo Arthur's Seat sall be my bed,
 The sheets sall ne'er be pressed by me ;
Saint Anton's Well sall be my drink ;
 Since my true love's forsaken me.
Martinmas wind, when wilt thou blaw,
 And shake the green leaves aff the tree ?
O gentle death, when wilt thou come ?
 For of my life I am wearie.

'Tis not the frost that freezes fell,
 Nor blawing snaw's inclemencie,
'Tis not sic cauld that makes me cry ;
 But my love's heart grown cauld to me.
When we cam' in by Glasgow toun,
 We were a comely sicht to see ;
My love was clad in the black velvet,
 An' I mysel' in cramasie.

But had I wist before I kiss'd
 .That love had been sae ill to win,
I'd lock'd my heart in a case o' gowd,
 And pinn'd it wi' a siller pin.
Oh, oh, if my young babe were born,
 And set upon the nurse's knee ;
And I mysel' were dead and gane,
 And the green grass growing over me !

UNKNOWN.

XXIV

BARBARA

ON the Sabbath-day,
Through the churchyard old and gray,
Over the crisp and yellow leaves I held my rustling way :
And amid the words of mercy, falling on my soul like
    balms,
'Mid the gorgeous storms of music—in the mellow organ-
    calms,
'Mid the upward-streaming prayers, and the rich and
    solemn psalms,
I stood careless, Barbara.

My heart was otherwhere
While the organ shook the air,
And the priest, with outspread hands, blest the people
    with a prayer ;
But, when rising to go homeward, with a mild and saint-
    like shine
Gleamed a face of airy beauty with its heavenly eyes on
    mine—
Gleamed and vanished in a moment—O that face was
    surely thine
Out of heaven, Barbara !

O pallid, pallid face !
O earnest eyes of grace !
When last I saw thee, dearest, it was in another place.
You came running forth to meet me with my love-gift on
    your wrist :
The flutter of a long white dress, then all was lost in
    mist—
A purple stain of agony was on the mouth I kissed,
That wild morning, Barbara.

I searched, in my despair,
Sunny noon and midnight air ;
I could not drive away the thought that you were lingering
        there.
O many and many a winter night I sat when you were
        gone,
My worn face buried in my hands, beside the fire alone—
Within the dripping churchyard, the rain plashing on the
        stone,
You were sleeping, Barbara.

'Mong angels, do you think
Of the precious golden link
I clasped around your happy arm while sitting by yon
        brink ?
Or when that night of gliding dance, of laughter and
        guitars,
Was emptied of its music, and we watched, through
        latticed bars,
The silent midnight heaven creeping o'er us with its stars,
Till the day broke, Barbara ?

In the years I've changed ;
Wild and far my heart hath ranged,
And many sins and errors now have been on me avenged ;
But to you I have been faithful, whatsoever good I lacked :
I loved you, and above my life still hangs that love intact—
Your love the trembling rainbow, I the reckless cataract—
Still I love you, Barbara.

Yet, love, I am unblest ;
With many doubts opprest,
I wander like a desert wind, without a place of rest.
Could I but win you for an hour from off that starry shore,

The hunger of my soul were stilled, for Death hath told
    you more
Than the melancholy world doth know; things deeper
    than all lore
You could teach me, Barbara.

In vain, in vain, in vain,
You will never come again.
There droops upon the dreary hills a mournful fringe of
    rain ;
The gloaming closes slowly round, loud winds are in the
    tree,
Round selfish shores for ever moans the hurt and wounded
    sea,
There is no rest upon the earth, peace is with death and
    thee, Barbara.

                       ALEXANDER SMITH.

XXV

·BERTRAM AND HELENA

I AM undone : there is no living, none,
If Bertram be away.   It were all one
That I should love a bright particular star,
And think to wed it, he is so above me :
In his bright radiance and collateral light
Must I be comforted, not in his sphere.
The ambition in my love thus plagues itself :
The hind, that would be mated with the lion,
Must die for love.   'Twas pretty, though a plague,
To see him every hour ; to sit and draw
His arched brows, his hawking eye, his curls,

In our heart's table ; heart, too capable
Of every line and trick of his sweet favour :
But now he's gone, and my idolatrous fancy
Must sanctify his relics.

·   WILLIAM SHAKESPEARE.

XXVI

TOO LATE

EACH on his own strict line we move,
And some find death ere they find love ;
So far apart their lives are thrown
From the twin soul which halves their own.

And sometimes, by still harder fate,
The lovers meet, but meet too late.
—Thy heart is mine !—*True, true ! ah, true !*
—Then, love, thy hand !—*Ah no ! adieu !*

MATTHEW ARNOLD.

XXVII

HIGHLAND MARY

YE banks and braes and streams around
    The castle o' Montgomery,
Green be your woods, and fair your flowers,
    Your waters never drumlie !
There simmer first unfaulds her robes,
    And there they langest tarry ;
For there I took the last farewéll
    O' my sweet Highland Mary.

How sweetly bloom'd the gay green birk,
    How rich the hawthorn's blossom,
As underneath their fragrant shade
    I clasp'd her to my bosom !
The golden hours, on angel wings,
    Flew o'er me and my dearie ;
For dear to me, as light and life,
    Was my sweet Highland Mary.

Wi' mony a vow, and lock'd embrace,
    Our parting was fu' tender ;
And pledging aft to meet again
    We tore oursels asunder ;
But oh ! fell death's untimely frost,
    That nipt my flower sae early !
Now green's the sod and cauld's the clay
    That wraps my Highland Mary.

O pale, pale now, those rosy lips,
    I aft hae kissed sae fondly !
And closed for aye the sparkling glance
    That dwelt on me sae kindly !
And mouldering now in silent dust,
    That heart that lo'ed me dearly !
But still within my bosom's core
    Shall live my Highland Mary.
                    ROBERT BURNS.

XXVIII

CLOISTERED LOVE

(Eloisa to Abelard)

How happy is the blameless vestal's lot !
The world forgetting, by the world forgot :
Eternal sunshine of the spotless mind !
Each prayer accepted, and each wish resign'd ;
Labour and rest, that equal periods keep ;
Obedient slumbers that can wake and weep ;
Desires compos'd, affections ever even ;
Tears that delight, and sighs that waft to Heaven.
Grace shines around her with serenest beams,
And whispering angels prompt her golden dreams.
For her the unfading rose of Eden blooms,
And wings of seraphs shed divine perfumes ;
For her the spouse prepares the bridal ring ;
For her, white virgins hymeneals sing ;
To sounds of heavenly harps she dies away,
And melts in visions of eternal day.

Far other dreams my erring soul employ,
Far other raptures of unholy joy :
When at the close of each sad, sorrowing day,
Fancy restores what vengeance snatch'd away,
Then conscience sleeps, and leaving nature free,
All my loose soul unbounded springs to thee.
                              Alexander Pope.

XXIX

TO MARY IN HEAVEN

THOU lingering star, with lessening ray,
  That lov'st to greet the early morn,
Again thou usher'st in the day
  My Mary from my soul was torn.
O Mary ! dear departed shade !
  Where is thy place of blissful rest ?
Seest thou thy lover lowly laid ?
  Hear'st thou the groans that rend his breast ?

That sacred hour can I forget ?
  Can I forget the hallowed grove,
Where by the winding Ayr we met,
  To live one day of parting love ?
Eternity will not efface
  Those records dear of transports past ;
Thy image at our last embrace ;
  Ah ! little thought we 't was our last !

Ayr, gurgling, kissed his pebbled shore,
  O'erhung with wild woods, thickening green ;
The fragrant birch and hawthorn hoar
  Twined amorous round the raptured scene.
The flowers sprang wanton to be pressed,
  The birds sang love on every spray,
Till too, too soon, the glowing west
  Proclaimed the speed of winged day.

Still o'er these scenes my memory wakes,
  And fondly broods with miser care !
Time but the impression deeper makes,
  As streams their channels deeper wear.

My Mary, dear departed shade!
  Where is thy blissful place of rest?
Seest thou thy lover lowly laid?
  Hear'st thou the groans that rend his breast?
ROBERT BURNS.

XXX

THE LASS OF LOCHROYAN

" O wha will shoe my bonny foot?
  And wha will glove my hand?
And wha will lace my middle jimp
  Wi' a lang, lang linen band?

" O wha will kame my yellow hair
  With a new-made silver kame?
And wha will father my young son
  Till Lord Gregory come hame?"

" Thy father will shoe thy bonny foot,
  Thy mother will glove thy hand,
Thy sister will lace thy middle jimp,
  Till Lord Gregory come to land.

" Thy brother will kame thy yellow hair
  With a new-made silver kame,
And God will be thy bairn's father
  Till Lord Gregory come hame."

" But I will get a bonny boat,
  And I will sail the sea;
And I will gang to Lord Gregory,
  Since he canna come hame to me."

Syne she's gar'd build a bonny boat,
    To sail the salt, salt sea:
The sails were o' the light green silk,
    The tows[1] o' taffety.

She hadna sailed but twenty leagues,
    But twenty leagues and three,
When she met wi' a rank robber,
    And a' his company.

"Now whether are ye the queen hersell
    (For so ye weel might be),
Or are ye the lass o' Lochroyan,
    Seekin' Lord Gregory?"

"O I am neither the queen," she said,
    "Nor sic I seem to be;
But I am the lass of Lochroyan,
    Seekin' Lord Gregory."

"O see na thou yon bonny bower,
    It's a' covered o'er wi' tin?
When thou hast sailed it round about,
    Lord Gregory is within."

And when she saw the stately tower
    Shining sae clear and bright,
Whilk stood aboon the jawing[2] wave,
    Built on a rock of height,

Says—"Row the boat, my mariners,
    And bring me to the land!
For yonder I see my love's castle
    Close by the salt sea strand."

1 *Tows*—ropes.   2 *Jawing*—dashing.

D

She sailed it round, and sailed it round,
    And loud, loud cried she—
" Now break, now break, ye fairy charms,
    And set my true love free !"

She's ta'en her young son in her arms,
    And to the door she's gane ;
And long she knocked, and sair she ca'd,
    But answer got she nane.

" O open the door, Lord Gregory !
    O open, and let me in !
For the wind blaws through my yellow hair,
    And the rain draps o'er my chin."

" Awa, awa, ye ill woman !
    Ye're no come here for good !
Ye're but some witch, or wil' warlock,
    Or mermaid o' the flood."

" I am neither witch, nor wil' warlock,
    Nor mermaid o' the sea ;
But I am Annie of Lochroyan ;
    O open the door to me !"

" Gin thou be Annie of Lochroyan
    (As I trow thou binna she),
Now tell me some o' the love tokens .
    That past between thee and me."

" O dinna ye mind, Lord Gregory,
    As we sat at the wine,
We changed the rings frae our fingers,
    And I can show thee mine ?

" O yours was gude, and gude enough,
    But aye the best was mine ;
For yours was o' the gude red gowd,
    But mine o' the diamond fine.

" Now, open the door, Lord Gregory !
    Open the door, I pray !
For thy young son is in my arms,
    And will be dead ere day."

" If thou be the lass of Lochroyan
    (As I kenna thou be),
Tell me some mair o' the love tokens
    Past between me and thee."

Fair Annie turned her round about—
    " Weel, since that it be sae,
May never a woman, that has born a son,
    Hae a heart sae fou o' wae !

" Take down, take down that mast o' gowd !
    Set up a mast o' tree !
It disna become a forsaken lady
    To sail sae royallie."

When the cock had crawn, and the day did dawn,
    And the sun began to peep,
Then up and raise him Lord Gregory,
    And sair, sair did he weep.

" Oh, I hae dreamed a dream, mother,
    I wish it may prove true !
That the bonny lass of Lochroyan
    Was at the yate e'en now.

" Oh, I hae dreamed a dream, mother,
  The thought o't gars me greet !
That fair Annie of Lochroyan
  Lay cauld dead at my feet."

" Gin it be for Annie of Lochroyan
  That ye make a' this din,
She stood a' last night at your door,
  But I trow she wan na in."

" O wae betide ye, ill woman !
  An ill deid may ye dee !
That wadna open the door to her,
  Nor yet wad waken me."

O he's gane down to yon shore side
  As fast as he could fare ;
He saw fair Annie in the boat,
  But the wind it tossed her sair.

" And hey, Annie, and how, Annie !
  O Annie, winna ye bide ?"
But aye the mair he cried " Annie,"
  The braider grew the tide.

" And hey, Annie, and how, Annie !
  Dear Annie, speak to me !"
But aye the louder he cried " Annie,"
  The louder roared the sea.

The wind blew loud, the sea grew rough,
  And dashed the boat on shore ;
Fair Annie floated through the faem,
  But the babie raise no more.

LOVE'S TRAGEDIES

Lord Gregory tore his yellow hair,
   And made a heavy moan ;
Fair Annie's corpse lay at his feet,
   Her bonny young son was gone.

O cherry, cherry was her cheek,
   And gowden was her hair ;
But clay-cold were her rosy lips—
   Nae spark o' life was there.

And first he kissed her cherry cheek,
   And syne he kissed her chin,
And syne he kissed her rosy lips—
   There was nae breath within.

" O wae betide my cruel mother !
   An ill death may she die !
She turned my true love frae my door,
   Wha came sae far to me.

" O wae betide my cruel mother,
   An ill death may she die !
She turned fair Annie frae my door,
   Wha died for love o' me."

UNKNOWN.

ROMANCE OF LOVE

> The faery power
> Of unreflecting love.
>
> KEATS.

LOVE

ALL thoughts, all passions, all delights,
Whatever stirs this mortal frame,
All are but ministers of Love,
    And feed his sacred flame.

Oft in my waking dreams do I
Live o'er again that happy hour,
When midway on the mount I lay,
    Beside the ruin'd tower.

The moonshine, stealing o'er the scene,
Had blended with the lights of eve ;
And she was there, my hope, my joy,
    My own dear Genevieve !

She lean'd against the armed man,
The statue of the armed knight ;
She stood and listen'd to my lay,
    Amid the lingering light.

Few sorrows hath she of her own,
My hope ! my joy ! my Genevieve !
She loves me best, whene'er I sing
    The songs that made her grieve.

I play'd a soft and doleful air,
I sang an old and moving story—
An old rude song, that suited well
    That ruin wild and hoary.

She listen'd with a flitting blush,
With downcast eyes and modest grace ;
For well she knew I could not choose
    But gaze upon her face.

I told her of the knight that wore
Upon his shield a burning brand ;
And that for ten long years he woo'd
    The Lady of the Land.

I told her how he pined ; and ah !
The deep, the low, the pleading tone
With which I sang another's love,
    Interpreted my own.

She listen'd with a flitting blush,
With downcast eyes and modest grace ;
And she forgave me that I gazed
    Too fondly on her face !

But when I told the cruel scorn
That crazed that bold and lovely knight,
And that he crossed the mountain-woods,
    Nor rested day nor night ;

That sometimes from the savage den,
And sometimes from the darksome shade,
And sometimes starting up at once
    In green and sunny glade,—

There came and look'd him in the face
An angel beautiful and bright ;
And that he knew it was a fiend,
  This miserable knight !

And that, unknowing what he did,
He leap'd amid a murderous band,
And saved from outrage worse than death
  The Lady of the Land ;—

And how she wept, and clasp'd his knees ;
And how she tended him in vain ;
And ever strove to expiate
  The scorn that crazed his brain ;—

And that she nursed him in a cave ;
And how his madness went away,
When on the yellow forest leaves
  A dying man he lay ;—

His dying words—but when I reach'd
That tenderest strain of all the ditty,
My faltering voice and pausing harp
  Disturb'd her soul with pity !

All impulses of soul and sense
Had thrill'd my guileless Genevieve ;
The music and the doleful tale,
  The rich and balmy eve ;

And hopes, and fears that kindle hope,
An undistinguishable throng,
And gentle wishes, long subdued,
  Subdued and cherish'd long !

She wept with pity and delight,
She blush'd with love, and virgin shame ;
And like the murmur of a dream,
　I heard her breathe my name.

Her bosom heaved—she stepped aside ;
As conscious of my look she stept ;
Then suddenly, with timorous eye,
　She fled to me and wept.

She half inclosed me with her arms,
She press'd me with a meek embrace ;
And bending back her head, look'd up,
　And gazed upon my face.

'Twas partly love, and partly fear,
And partly 'twas a bashful art,
That I might rather feel, than see,
　The swelling of her heart.

I calm'd her fears, and she was calm,
And told her love with virgin pride ;
And so I won my Genevieve,
　My bright and beauteous bride.
　　　　　SAMUEL TAYLOR COLERIDGE.

XXXII

LOVE THE LORD OF ALL

(ALBERT GRÆME'S SONG)

IT was an English ladye bright
　(The sun shines fair on Carlisle wall),
And she would marry a Scottish knight,
　For Love will still be lord of all.

Blithely they saw the rising sun,
　　When he shone fair on Carlisle wall,
But they were sad ere day was done,
　　Though Love was still the lord of all.

Her sire gave brooch and jewel fine,
　　Where the sun shines fair on Carlisle wall ;
Her brother gave but a flask of wine,
　　For ire that Love was lord of all.

For she had lands, both meadow and lea,
　　Where the sun shines fair on Carlisle wall,
And he swore her death, ere he would see
　　A Scottish knight the lord of all !

That wine she had not tasted well
　　('The sun shines fair on Carlisle wall),
When dead, in her true love's arms, she fell,
　　For Love was still the lord of all.

He pierced her brother to the heart,
　　Where the sun shines fair on Carlisle wall ;
So perish all would true love part,
　　That Love may still be lord of all.

And then he took the cross divine,
　　Where the sun shines fair on Carlisle wall ;
And died for her sake in Palestine ;
　　So Love was still the lord of all.
　　　　　　　　　　SIR WALTER SCOTT.

XXXIII

SHELLEY AND EMILIA

THE day is come, and thou wilt fly with me.
To whatsoe'er of dull mortality
Is mine, remain a vestal sister still ;
To the intense, the deep, the imperishable,
Not mine but me, henceforth be thou united
Even as a bride, delighting and delighted.
The hour is come :—the destined Star has risen
Which shall descend upon a vacant prison.
The walls are high, the gates are strong, thick set
The sentinels—but true love never yet
Was thus constrained : it overleaps all fence :
Like lightning, with invisible violence
Piercing its continents ; like Heaven's free breath,
Which he who grasps can hold not ; liker Death,
Who rides upon a thought, and makes his way
Through temple, tower, and palace, and the array
Of arms : more strength has Love than he or they ;
For it can burst his charnel, and make free
The limbs in chains, the heart in agony,
The soul in dust and chaos.
                              Emily,
A ship is floating in the harbour now,
A wind is hovering o'er the mountain's brow ;
There is a path on the sea's azure floor,
No keel has ever ploughed that path before ;
The halcyons brood around the foamless isles ;
The treacherous Ocean has forsworn its wiles ;
The merry mariners are bold and free :
Say, my heart's sister, wilt thou sail with me ?
Our bark is as an albatross, whose nest
Is a far Eden of the purple East ;

And we between her wings will sit, while Night
And Day, and Storm and Calm, pursue their flight,
Our ministers, along the boundless Sea,
Treading each other's heels, unheededly.
                    PERCY BYSSHE SHELLEY.

XXXIV

MY BONNY MARY

Go fetch to me a pint o' wine,
    And fill it in a silver tassie;
That I may drink, before I go,
    A service to my bonnie lassie.
The boat rocks at the pier o' Leith;
    Fu' loud the wind blaws frae the ferry;
The ship rides by the Berwick-law,
    And I maun leave my bonny Mary.

The trumpets sound, the banners fly,
    The glittering spears are rankèd ready;
The shouts o' war are heard afar,
    The battle closes thick and bloody;
But it's not the roar o' sea or shore
    Wad mak' me langer wish to tarry;
Nor shout o' war that's heard afar,—
    It's leaving thee, my bonny Mary!
                    ROBERT BURNS.

XXXV

BALLAD OF THE BIRD-BRIDE

(ESKIMO)

THEY never come back, though I loved them well;
    I watch the South in vain;
The snow-bound skies are blear and gray,
Waste and wide is the wild gull's way,
    And she comes never again.

Years agone, on the flat, white strand,
    I won my sweet sea-girl:
Wrapped in my coat of the snow-white fur,
I watched the wild birds settle and stir,
    The gray gulls gather and whirl.

One, the greatest of all the flock,
    Perched on an ice-floe bare,
Called and cried as her heart were broke,
And straight they were changed, that fleet bird-folk,
    To women young and fair.

Swift I sprang from my hiding-place,
    And held the fairest fast;
I held her fast, the sweet, strange thing:
Her comrades skirled, but they all took wing,
    And smote me as they passed.

I bore her safe to my warm snow house;
    Full sweetly there she smiled;
And yet, whenever the shrill winds blew,
She would beat her long white arms anew,
    And her eyes glanced quick and wild.

But I took her to wife, and clothed her warm
  With skins of the gleaming seal ;
Her wandering glances sank to rest
When she held a babe to her fair, warm breast,
  And she loved me dear and leal.

Together we tracked the fox and the seal,
  And at her behest I swore
That bird and beast my bow might slay
For meat and for raiment, day by day,
  But never a gray gull more.

A weariful watch I kept for aye
  'Mid the snow and the changeless frost :
Woe is me for my broken word !
Woe, woe's me for my bonny bird,
  My bird and the love-time lost !

Have ye forgotten the old keen life?
  The hut with the skin-strewn floor?
O winged white wife, and children three,
Is there no room left in your hearts for me,
  Or our home on the low sea-shore?

Once the quarry was scarce and shy,
  Sharp hunger gnawed us sore,
My spoken oath was clean forgot,
My bow twanged thrice with a swift, straight shot,
  And slew me sea-gulls four.

The sun hung red on the sky's dull breast,
  The snow was wet and red ;
Her voice shrilled out in a woeful cry,
She beat her long white arms on high,
  "The hour is here," she said.

F.

She beat her arms, and she cried full fain
  As she swayed and wavered there.
" Fetch me the feathers, my children three,
Feathers and plumes for you and me,
  Bonny gray wings to wear ! "

They ran to her side, our children three,
  With the plumage black and gray ;
Then she bent her down and drew them near,
She laid the plumes on our children dear,
  'Mid the snow and the salt sea-spray.

" Babes of mine, of the wild wind's kin,
  Feather ye quick, nor stay.
Oh, oho ! but the wild winds blow !
Babes of mine, it is time to go :
  Up, dear hearts, and away ! "

And lo ! the gray plumes covered them all,
  Shoulder and breast and brow.
I felt the wind of their whirling flight :
Was it sea or sky ? was it day or night ?
  It is always night-time now.

Dear, will you never relent, come back ?
  I loved you long and true.
O winged white wife, and our children three,
Of the wild wind's kin though ye surely be,
  Are ye not of my kin too ?

Ay, ye once were mine, and, till I forget,
  Ye are mine for ever and aye,
Mine, wherever your wild wings go,
While shrill winds whistle across the snow
  And the skies are blear and gray.

                GRAHAM ROSAMUND TOMSON.

XXXVI

JOCK OF HAZELDEAN

" WHY weep ye by the tide, ladie?
   Why weep ye by the tide?
I'll wed ye to my youngest son,
   And ye sall be his bride :
And ye sall be his bride, ladie,
   Sae comely to be seen "—
But aye she loot the tears down fa',
   For Jock of Hazeldean.

" Now let this wilful grief be done,
   And dry that cheek so pale ;
Young Frank is chief of Errington,
   And lord of Langley-dale ;
His step is first in peaceful ha',
   His sword in battle keen "—
But aye she loot the tears down fa',
   For Jock of Hazeldean.

" A chain o' gold ye sall not lack,
   Nor braid to bind your hair ;
Nor mettled hound, nor managed hawk,
   Nor palfrey fresh and fair ;
And you, the foremost o' them a',
   Shall ride our forest queen "—
But aye she loot the tears down fa',
   For Jock of Hazeldean.

The kirk was deck'd at morning-tide,
　　The tapers glimmer'd fair ;
The priest and bridegroom wait the bride,
　　And dame and knight are there.
They sought her both by bower and ha',
　　The ladie was not seen !
She's o'er the Border, and awa
　　Wi' Jock of Hazeldean.
　　　　　　　　　SIR WALTER SCOTT.

.

XXXVII

THE INDIAN SERENADE

I ARISE from dreams of thee
In the first sweet sleep of night,
When the winds are breathing low,
And the stars are shining bright :
I arise from dreams of thee,
And a spirit in my feet
Hath led me—who knows how?
To thy chamber window, Sweet !

The wandering airs they faint
On the dark, the silent stream—
And the Champak's odours fail
Like sweet thoughts in a dream ;
The nightingale's complaint,
It dies upon her heart ;—
As I must on thine,
O ! belovèd as thou art !

O lift me from the grass !
I die ! I faint ! I fail !
Let thy love in kisses rain
On my lips and eyelids pale.
My cheek is cold and white, alas !
My heart beats loud and fast ;—
Oh ! press it close to thine again,
Where it will break at last.

PERCY BYSSHE SHELLEY.

XXXVIII

LADY HERON'S SONG

O, YOUNG Lochinvar is come out of the west,
Through all the wide border his steed was the best ;
And save his good broad-sword, he weapon had none,
He rode all unarmed, and he rode all alone.
So faithful in love, and so dauntless in war,
There never was knight like the young Lochinvar.

He stayed not for brake, and he stopped not for stone,
He swam the Esk river where ford there was none ;
But, ere he alighted at Netherby gate,
The bride had consented, the gallant came late :
For a laggard in love, and a dastard in war,
Was to wed the fair Ellen of brave Lochinvar.

So boldly he entered the Netherby Hall,
Among bride's-men, and kinsmen, and brothers, and all :
Then spake the bride's father, his hand on his sword
(For the poor craven bridegroom said never a word),
" O come ye in peace here, or come ye in war,
Or to dance at our bridal, young Lord Lochinvar ? "

"I long wooed your daughter, my suit you denied ;—
Love swells like the Solway, but ebbs like its tide—
And now am I come, with this lost love of mine,
To lead but one measure, drink one cup of wine.
There are maidens in Scotland more lovely by far,
That would gladly be bride to the young Lochinvar."

The bride kissed the goblet ; the knight took it up,
He quaffed off the wine, and he threw down the cup.
She looked down to blush, and she looked up to sigh,
With a smile on her lips, and a tear in her eye.
He took her soft hand, ere her mother could bar,—
"Now tread we a measure !" said young Lochinvar.

So stately his form, and so lovely her face,
That never a hall such a galliard did grace ;
While her mother did fret, and her father did fume,
And the bridegroom stood dangling his bonnet and
     plume ;
And the bride-maidens whispered, "'Twere better by
     far
To have matched our fair cousin with young Loch-
     invar."

One touch to her hand, and one word in her ear,
When they reached the hall door, and the charger stood
     near ;
So light to the croupe the fair lady he swung,
So light to the saddle before her he sprung !
"She is won ! we are gone, over bank, bush, and scaur ;
They'll have fleet steeds that follow," quoth young
     Lochinvar.

There was mounting 'mong Græmes of the Netherby
     clan ;

Forsters, Fenwicks, and Musgraves, they rode and they
    ran :
There was racing and chasing, on Cannobie Lea,
But the lost bride of Netherby ne'er did they see.
So daring in love, and so dauntless in war,
Have ye e'er heard of gallant like young Lochinvar ?
                    SIR WALTER SCOTT.

XXXIX

LORD ULLIN'S DAUGHTER

A CHIEFTAIN, to the Highlands bound,
    Cries, "Boatman, do not tarry !
And I'll give thee a silver pound
    To row us o'er the ferry."

"Now who be ye, would cross Lochgyle,
    This dark and stormy water?"
"O, I'm the chief of Ulva's isle,
    And this Lord Ullin's daughter.

"And fast before her father's men
    Three days we've fled together,
For should he find us in the glen,
    My blood would stain the heather.

"His horsemen hard behind us ride ;
    Should they our steps discover,
Then who will cheer my bonny bride
    When they have slain her lover?"

Outspoke the hardy Highland wight,
    "I'll go, my chief—I'm ready :
It is not for your silver bright,
    But for your winsome lady :

" And by my word, the bonny bird
    In danger shall not tarry :
So though the waves are raging white,
    I'll row you o'er the ferry."

By this the storm grew loud apace,
    The water-wraith was shrieking ;
And in the scowl of Heaven each face
    Grew dark as they were speaking.

But still as wilder blew the wind,
    And as the night grew drearer,
Adown the glen rode armèd men,
    Their trampling sounded nearer. ·

" O haste thee, haste ! " the lady cries,
    " Though tempests round us gather ;
I'll meet the raging of the skies,
    But not an angry father."

The boat has left a stormy land,
    A stormy sea before her,—
When, oh ! too strong for human hand,
    The tempest gathered o'er her.

And still they row'd amidst the roar
    Of waters fast prevailing :
Lord Ullin reach'd that fatal shore,
    His wrath was changed to wailing.

For sore dismay'd, through storm and shade,
    His child he did discover ;—
One lovely hand she stretched for aid,
    And one was round her lover.

" Come back, come back ! " he cried in grief,
    " Across this stormy water :
And I'll forgive your Highland chief,
    My daughter !—O my daughter ! "

'Twas vain :—the loud waves lash'd the shore,
    Return or aid preventing :—
The waters wild went o'er his child,
    And he was left lamenting.
                  THOMAS CAMPBELL.

XL

THE DEMON-LOVER

" O WHERE have you been, my long lost love,
    This seven long years and more ? "
" O I'm come to seek my former vows
    Ye granted me before."

" O hold your tongue of your former vows,
    For they will breed sad strife ;
O hold your tongue of your former vows,
    For I am become a wife."

He turned him right and round about,
    And the tear blinded his e'e ;
" I wad never hae trodden on Irish ground
    If it had not been for thee.

" I might hae had a king's daughter,
    Far, far beyond the sea ;
I might hae had a king's daughter,
    Had it not been for love o' thee."

" If ye might have had a king's daughter,
    Yersel ye had to blame ;
Ye might have taken the king's daughter,
    For ye kenned that I was nane."

" O fause are the vows of womankind,
    But fair is their fause bodie ;
I never wad hae trodden on Irish ground,
    Had it not been for love o' thee."

" If I was to leave my husband dear,
    And my two babes also,
O what have you to take me to,
    If with you I should go ? "

" I hae seven ships upon the sea,
    The eighth brought me to land ;
With four-and-twenty bold mariners,
    And music on every hand."

She has taken up her two little babes,
    Kissed them baith cheek and chin ;
" O fair ye weel, my ain two babes,
    For I'll never see you again."

She set her foot upon the ship,
    No mariners could she behold ;
But the sails were o' the taffetie,
    And the masts o' the beaten gold.

She had not sailed a league, a league,
    A league but barely three,
When dismal grew his countenance,
    And drumlie grew his e'e.

The masts, that were like the beaten gold,
    Bent not on the heaving seas ;
The sails, that were o' the taffetic,
    Fill'd not in the east land breeze.

They had not sailed a league, a league,
    A league but barely three,
Until she espied his cloven foot,
    And she wept right bitterlie.

" O hold your tongue of your weeping," says he,
    " Of your weeping now let me be ;
I will show you how the lilies grow
    On the banks of Italy."

" O what are yon, yon pleasant hills,
    That the sun shines sweetly on ? "
" O yon are the hills of heaven," he said,
    " Where you will never win."

" O whaten a mountain is yon," she said,
    " All so dreary wi' frost and snow ? "
" O yon is the mountain of hell," he said,
    " Where you and I will go."

And aye when she turned her round about,
    Aye taller he seemed for to be ;
Until that the tops o' that gallant ship
    Nae taller were than he.

The clouds grew dark, and the wind grew loud,
    And the levin filled her e'e ;
And waesome wail'd the snow-white sprites
    Upon the gurlie sea.

He strack the tap-mast wi' his hand,
  The foremast wi' his knee;
And he brake that gallant ship in twain,
  And sank her in the sea.

                    UNKNOWN.

XLI

LEWTI,

OR THE CIRCASSIAN LOVE-CHANT

AT midnight by the stream I roved,
To forget the form I loved.
Image of Lewti! from my mind
Depart; for Lewti is not kind.

The moon was high, the moonlight gleam,
  And the shadow of a star,
Heaved upon Tamaha's stream;
  But the rock shone brighter far.
The rock half-shelter'd from my view
By pendent boughs of tressy yew.
So shines my Lewti's forehead fair,
Gleaming through her sable hair.
Image of Lewti! from my mind
Depart; for Lewti is not kind.

I saw a cloud of palest hue, —
  Onward to the moon it passed:
Still brighter and more bright it grew,
With floating colours not a few,
  Till it reach'd the moon at last;

Then the cloud was wholly bright,
With a rich and amber light !
And so with many a hope I seek,
   And with such joy I find my Lewti ;
And even so my pale wan cheek
   Drinks in as deep a flush of beauty !
Nay, treacherous image ! leave my mind,
If Lewti never will be kind.

The little cloud—it floats away,
   Away it goes ; away so soon ?
Alas ! it has no power to stay :
Its hues are dim, its hues are gray—
   Away it passes from the moon !
How mournfully it seems to fly,
   Ever fading more and more,
To joyless regions of the sky—
   And now 'tis whiter than before !
As white as my poor cheek will be,
   When, Lewti ! on my couch I lie
A dying man for love of thee.
Nay, treacherous image ! leave my mind—
And yet, thou did'st not look unkind.

   I saw a vapour in the sky,
   Thin and white, and very high :
I ne'er beheld so thin a cloud.
   Perhaps the breezes, that can fly
   Now below and now above,
Have snatch'd aloft the lawny shroud
   Of lady fair—that died for love.
For maids, as well as youths, have perish'd
From fruitless love too fondly cherish'd.
Nay, treacherous image ! leave my mind—
For Lewti never will be kind.

Hush ! my heedless feet from under,
  Slip the crumbling banks for ever :
Like echoes to a distant thunder,
  They plunge into the gentle river.
The river-swans have heard my tread,
And startle from their reedy bed.
O beauteous birds ! methinks ye measure
  Your movements to some heavenly tune !
O beauteous birds ! 'tis such a pleasure
  To see you move beneath the moon,
I would it were your true delight
To sleep by day and wake by night.

I know the place where Lewti lies,
When silent night has closed her eyes ;
  It is a breezy jasmine-bower,
.The nightingale sings o'er her head :
  Voice of the night, had I the power
That leafy labyrinth to thread,
And creep, like thee, with soundless tread,
I then might view her bosom white
Heaving lovely to my sight,
As these two swans together heave
On the gently-swelling wave.
Oh ! that she saw me in a dream,
  And dreamt that I had died for care !
All pale and wasted I would seem,
  Yet fair withal, as spirits are !
I'd die indeed, if I might see
Her bosom heave, and heave for me !
Soothe, gentle image ! soothe my mind !
To-morrow Lewti may be kind.

                    SAMUEL TAYLOR COLERIDGE.

XLII

THE GAY GOSS HAWK

" O WALY, waly, my gay goss hawk,
    Gin your feathering be sheen !"
" And waly, waly, my master dear,
    Gin ye look pale and lean.

" O have ye tint, at tournament,
    Your sword, or yet your spear?
Or mourn ye for the Southern lass,
    Whom ye may not win near?"

" I have not tint, at tournament,
    My sword nor yet my spear;
But sair I mourn for my true love,
    Wi' mony a bitter tear.

" But weel's me on ye, my gay goss hawk,
    Ye can baith speak and flee;
Ye sall carry a letter to my love,
    Bring an answer back to me."

" But how sall I your true love find,
    Or how suld I her know?
I bear a tongue ne'er wi' her spake,
    An eye that ne'er her saw."

" O weel sall ye my true love ken,
    Sae sune as ye her see;
For of a' the flowers of fair England,
    The fairest flower is she.

" The red that's on my true love's cheek,
    Is like blood-drops on the snaw ;
The white that is on her breast bare,
    Like the down o' the white sea-maw.

" And even at my love's bour door
    There grows a flowering birk ;
And ye maun sit and sing thereon
    As she gangs to the kirk.

" And four-and-twenty fair ladyes
    Will to the mass repair ;
But weel may ye my ladye ken,
    The fairest ladye there."

Lord William has written a love-letter,
    Put it under his pinion gray ;
And he is awa' to Southern land,
    As fast as wings can gae.

And even at that ladye's bour
    There grew a flowering birk ;
And he sat down and sung thereon
    As she gaed to the kirk.

And weel he kent that ladye fair
    Amang her maidens free ;
For the flower, that springs in May morning,
    Was not sae sweet as she.

He lighted at the ladye's yate,
    And sat him on a pin ;
And sang fu' sweet the notes o' love,
    Till a' was cosh [1] within.

<hr>

[1] *Cosh*—quiet.

And first he sang a low, low note,
   And syne he sang a clear ;
And aye the o'erword o' the sang
   Was—" Your love can no win here."

" Feast on, feast on, my maidens a',
   The wine flows you amang,
While I gang to my shot-window,
   And hear yon bonny bird's sang.

" Sing on, sing on, my bonny bird,
   The sang ye sung yestreen ;
For weel I ken, by your sweet singing,
   Ye are frae my true love sen."

O first he sang a merry song,
   And syne he sang a grave ;
And syne he peck'd his feathers gray,
   To her the letter gave.

" Have there a letter from Lord William ;
   He says he's sent ye three.
He canna wait your love langer,
   But for your sake he'll dee."

" Gae bid him bake his bridal bread,
   And brew his bridal ale ;
And I shall meet him at Mary's Kirk,
   Lang, lang ere it be stale."

The ladye's gane to her chamber,
   And a moanfu' woman was she ;
As gin she had ta'en a sudden brash,[1]
   And were about to dee.

[1] *Brash*—sickness.

F

" A boon, a boon, my father deir,
    A boon I beg of thee ! "
" Ask not that paughty Scottish lord,
    For him you ne'er shall see.

" But, for your honest asking else,
    Weel granted it shall be."
" Then, gin I die in Southern land,
    In Scotland gar bury me.

" And the first kirk that ye come to,
    Ye's gar the mass be sung ;
And the next kirk that ye come to,
    Ye's gar the bells be rung.

" And when ye come to St. Mary's Kirk,
    Ye's tarry there till night."
And so her father pledged his word,
    And so his promise plight.

She has ta'en her to her bigly bour
    As fast as she could fare ;
And she has drank a sleepy draught,
    That she had mixed wi' care.

And pale, pale grew her rosy cheek,
    That was sae bright of blee,
And she seemed to be as surely dead
    As any one could be.

Then spak' her cruel step-minnie,
    " Tak' ye the burning lead,
And drap a drap on her bosome,
    To try if she be dead."

They took a drap o' boiling lead,
 They drapp'd it on her breast.
" Alas ! alas ! " her father cried,
 " She's dead without the priest."

She neither chattered with her teeth,
 Nor shivered with her chin.
" Alas ! alas ! " her father cried,
 " There is nae breath within."

Then up arose her seven brethren,
 And hew'd to her a bier ;
They hew'd it frae the solid aik,
 Laid it o'er wi' siller clear.

Then up and gat her seven sisters,
 And sew'd to her a kell ;
And every steek that they put in
 Sew'd to a siller bell.

The first Scots kirk that they cam' to,
 They gar'd the bells be rung.
The next Scots kirk that they cam' to,
 They gar'd the mass be sung.

But when they cam' to Saint Mary's Kirk,
 There stude spearmen all on a raw ;
And up and started Lord William,
 The chieftain amang them a'.

" Set down, set down the bier," he said ;
 " Let me look her upon : "
But as soon as Lord William touched her hand,
 Her colour began to come.

She brightened like the lily flower,
   Till her pale colour was gone ;
With rosy cheik, and ruby lip,
   She smiled her love upoh.

" A morsel of your bread, my lord,
   And one glass of your wine ;
For I hae fasted these three lang days,
   All for your sake and mine.

" Gae hame, gae hame, my seven bauld brothers,
   Gae hame and blaw your horn !
I trow ye wad hae gi'en me the skaith,
   But I've gi'en you the scorn.

" Commend me to my gray father,
   That wish'd my saul gude rest ;
But wae be to my cruel step-dame,
   Gar'd burn me on the breast."

UNKNOWN.

XLIII

JUAN AND HAIDÉE

IT was the cooling hour, just when the rounded
   Red sun sinks down behind the azure hill,
Which then seems as if the whole earth it bounded,
   Circling all nature, hush'd, and dim, and still,
With the far mountain-crescent half surrounded
   On one side, and the deep sea calm and chill
Upon the other, and the rosy sky,
With one star sparkling through it like an eye.

And thus they wander'd forth, and hand in hand,
  Over the shining pebbles and the shells,
Glided along the smooth and harden'd sand,
  And in the worn and wild receptacles
Work'd by the storms, yet work'd as it were plann'd,
  In hollow halls, with sparry roofs and cells,
They turn'd to rest ; and, each clasp'd by an arm,
Yielded to the deep twilight's purple charm.

They look'd up to the sky, whose floating glow
  Spread like a rosy ocean, vast and bright ;
They gazed upon the glittering sea below,
  Whence the broad moon rose circling into sight ;
They heard the wave's splash, and the wind so low,
  And saw each other's dark eyes darting light
Into each other—and, beholding this,
Their lips drew near, and clung into a kiss ;

A long, long kiss, a kiss of youth, and love,
  And beauty, all concentrating like rays
Into one focus, kindled from above ;
  Such kisses as belong to early days,
Where heart, and soul, and sense, in concert move,
  And the blood's lava, and the pulse a blaze,
Each kiss a heart-quake,—for a kiss's strength,
I think, it must be reckon'd by its length.

By length I mean duration ; theirs endured
  Heaven knows how long—no doubt ·they never
    reckon'd ;
And if they had, they could not have secured
  The sum of their sensations to a second :
They had not spoken ; but they felt allured,
  As if their souls and lips each other beckon'd,
Which, being join'd, like swarming bees they clung—
Their hearts the flowers from which the honey sprung.

They were alone, but not alone as they
   Who shut in chambers think it loneliness ;
The silent ocean, and the starlight bay,
   The twilight glow, which momently grew less,
The voiceless sands, and dropping caves, that lay
   Around them, made them to each other press,
As if there were no life beneath the sky
Save theirs, and that their life could never die.

They fear'd no eyes nor ears on that lone beach,
   They felt no terrors from the night, they were
All in all to each other : though their speech
   Was broken words, they *thought* a language there,—
And all the burning tongues the passions teach
   Found in one sigh the best interpreter
Of nature's oracle—first love,—that all
Which Eve has left her daughters since her fall.

Haidée spoke not of scruples, ask'd no vows,
   Nor offer'd any ; she had never heard
Of plight and promises to be a spouse,
   Or perils by a loving maid incurr'd ;
She was all which pure ignorance allows,
   And flew to her young mate like a young bird ;
And, never having dreamt of falsehood, she
Had not one word to say of constancy.

She loved, and was belovèd—she adored,
   And she was worshipp'd ; after nature's fashion,
Their intense souls, into each other pour'd,
   If souls could die, had perish'd in that passion,—
But by degrees their senses were restored,
   Again to be o'ercome, again to dash on ;
And, beating 'gainst *his* bosom, Haidée's heart
Felt as if never more to beat apart.

                GEORGE, LORD BYRON.

XLIV

LA BELLE DAME SANS MERCI

I

O WHAT can ail thee, knight-at-arms,
  Alone and palely loitering?
The sedge has withered from the lake,
  And no birds sing.

II

O what can ail thee, knight-at-arms,
  So haggard and so woe-begone?
The squirrel's granary is full,
  And the harvest's done.

III

I see a lily on thy brow
  With anguish moist and fever dew,
And on thy cheeks a fading rose
  Fast withereth too.

IV

I met a lady in the meads,
  Full beautiful—a faery's child,
Her hair was long, her foot was light,
  And her eyes were wild.

V

I made a garland for her head,
  And bracelets too, and fragrant zone ;
She look'd at me as she did love,
  And made sweet moan.

VI

I set her on my pacing steed,
  And nothing else saw all day long,
For sidelong would she bend, and sing
  A faery's song.

VII

She found me roots of relish sweet,
  And honey wild, and manna dew,
And sure in language strange she said—
  " I love thee true."

VIII

She took me to her elfin grot,
  And there she wept, and sigh'd full sore,
And there I shut her wild wild eyes
  With kisses four.

IX

And there she lulled me asleep,
  And there I dream'd—Ah ! woe betide
The latest dream I ever dream'd
  On the cold hill's side.

X

I saw pale kings and princes too,
  Pale warriors, death-pale were they all ;
They cried—" La Belle Dame sans Merci
  Hath thee in thrall."

XI

I saw their starved lips in the gloam,
  With horrid warning gaped wide,
And I awoke and found me here
  On the cold hill's side.

XII

And this is why I sojourn here,
  Alone and palely loitering,
Though the sedge is withered from the lake,
  And no birds sing.

JOHN KEATS.

LOVE'S PHILOSOPHY

Love is like understanding, that grows bright,
Gazing on many truths.

SHELLEY.

Sometimes thou seem'st not as thyself alone,
But as the meaning of all things that are.

D. G. ROSSETTI.

Gather, therefore, the rose while yet is prime,
For soon comes age, that will his pride deflower :
Gather the rose of love while yet is time.

SPENSER.

XLV

LOVE'S PHILOSOPHY

THE fountains mingle with the river,
   And the rivers with the ocean ;
The winds of heaven mix for ever
   With a sweet emotion ;
Nothing in the world is single ;
   All things by a law divine
In one another's being mingle ;—
   Why not I with thine ?

See the mountains kiss high heaven,
   And the waves clasp one another ;
No sister flower would be forgiven
   If it disdained its brother ;
And the sunlight clasps the earth,
   And the moonbeams kiss the sea :
What are all these kissings worth,
   If thou kiss not me ?

PERCY BYSSHE SHELLEY.

·

XLVI

LOVE THE IDEALIST

FOR love is a celestial harmony
Of likely hearts composed of stars' consent,
Which join together in sweet sympathy,
To work each other's joy and true content,
Which they have harboured since their first descent
Out of their heavenly bowers, where they did see
And know each other here belov'd to be.

Then wrong it were that any other twain
Should in love's gentle band combinèd be,
But those whom heaven did at first ordain,
And made out of one mould the more t' agree :
For all that like the beauty which they see
Straight do not love ; for love is not so light
As straight to burn at first beholder's sight.

But they which love indeed look otherwise
With pure regard and spotless true intent,
Drawing out of the object of their eyes
A more refinèd form, which they present
Unto their mind void of all blemishment ;
Which it reducing to her first perfection,
Beholdeth free from flesh's frail infection.

And then conforming it unto the light,
Which in itself it hath remaining still,
Of that first Sun, yet sparkling in his sight,
Thereof he fashions in his higher skill
An heavenly beauty to his fancy's will ;
And it embracing in his mind entire,
The mirror of his own thought doth admire.

Which seeing now so inly fair to be,
As outward it appeareth to the eye,
And with his spirit's proportion to agree,
He thereon fixeth all his fantasy,
And fully setteth his felicity ;
Counting it fairer than it is indeed,
And yet indeed her fairness doth exceed.

For lovers' eyes more sharply sighted be
Than other men's, and in dear love's delight
See more than any other eyes can see,
Through mutual receipt of beamës bright,
Which carry privy message to the sprite ;
And to their eyes that inmost fair display,
As plain as light discovers dawning day.

EDMUND SPENSER.

XLVII

TO DIANEME

SWEET, be not proud of those two eyes,
Which starlike sparkle in their skies ;
Nor be you proud, that you can see
All hearts your captives,—yours, yet free.
Be you not proud of that rich hair
Which wantons with the love-sick air :
Whenas that ruby which you wear,
Sunk from the tip of your soft ear,
Will last to be a precious stone
When all your world of beauty's gone.

ROBERT HERRICK.

XLVIII

LOOK, Delia, how we esteem the half-blown rose,
The image of thy blush and summer's honour,
Whilst yet her tender bud doth undisclose
That full of beauty, time bestows upon her.
No sooner spreads her glory in the air
But straight her wide blown pomp comes to decline:
She then is scorned that late adorned the Fair;
So fade the roses of those cheeks of thine.
No April can revive thy withered flowers
Whose springing grace adorns thy glory now:
Swift speedy Time, feathered with flying hours,
Dissolves the beauty of the fairest brow.
Then do not thou such treasure waste in vain,
But love now, whilst thou mayst be loved again.

SAMUEL DANIEL.

XLIX

I LOVED her for that she was beautiful;
And that to me she seemed to be all nature,
And all varieties of things in one:
Would set at night in clouds of tears, and rise
All light and laughter in the morning; fear
No petty customs nor appearances;
But think what others only dreamed about;
And say what others did but think; and do
What others would but say; and glory in
What others dared but do; so pure withal
In soul: in heart and act such conscious, yet
Such careless innocence, she made round her
A halo of delight; 'twas these which won me;—

And that she never schooled within her breast
One thought or feeling, but gave holiday
To all ; and that she made all even mine,
In the communion of love : and we
Grew like each other, for we loved each other ;
She, mild and generous as the air in Spring ;
And I, like Earth, all budding out with love.

PHILIP JAMES BAILEY.

L

SOUL, heart, and body, we thus singly name,
Are not, in love, divisible and distinct,
But each with each inseparably linked.
One is not honour, and the other shame,
But burn as closely fused as fuel, heat, and flame.

They do not love who give the body and keep
The heart ungiven ; nor they who yield the soul,
And guard the body.   Love doth give the whole ;
Its range being high as heaven, as ocean deep,
Wide as the realms of air or planet's curving sweep.

ALFRED AUSTIN.

LI

LOVE'S BLINDNESS

I HAVE heard of reasons manifold
  Why Love must needs be blind,
But this the best of all I hold,—
  His eyes are in his mind.

What outward form and feature are
  He guesseth but in part ;
But what within is good and fair
  He seeth with the heart.
                SAMUEL TAYLOR COLERIDGE.

LII

AMATURUS

SOMEWHERE beneath the sun,
  These quivering heart-strings prove it,
Somewhere there must be one
  Made for this soul, to move it ;
Some one that hides her sweetness
  From neighbours whom she slights,
Nor can attain completeness,
  Nor give her heart to rights ;
Some one whom I could court
  With no great change of manner,
Still holding reason's fort,
  Though waving fancy's banner ;
A lady, not so queenly
  As to disdain my hand,

Yet born to smile serenely
  Like those that rule the land ;
Noble, but not too proud ;
  With soft hair simply folded,
And bright face crescent-browed,
  And throat by Muses moulded ;
And eyelids lightly falling
  On little glistening seas,
Deep-calm, when gales are brawling,
  Though stirred by every breeze ;
Swift voice, like flight of dove
  Through minster-arches floating,
With sudden turns, when love
  Gets overnear to doting ;
Keen lips, that shape soft sayings
  Like crystals of the snow,
With pretty half-betrayings
  Of things one may not know ;
Fair hand, whose touches thrill,
  Like golden rod of wonder,
Which Hermes wields at will
  Spirit and flesh to sunder ;
Light foot, to press the stirrup
  In fearlessness and glee,
Or dance, till finches chirrup,
  And sink into the sea.
Forth, Love, and find this maid,
  Wherever she be hidden :
Speak,. Love, be not afraid,
  But plead as thou art bidden ;
And say, that he who taught thee
  His yearning want and pain,
Too dearly, dearly bought thee
  To part with thee in vain.
                    WILLIAM CORY.

LIII

ROUSSEAU'S LOVE

His love was passion's essence—as a tree
On fire by lightning ; with ethereal flame
Kindled he was, and blasted ; for to be
Thus, and enamour'd, were in him the same.
But his was not the love of living dame,
Nor of the dead who rise upon our dreams,
But of ideal beauty, which became
In him existence, and o'erflowing teems
Along his burning page, distemper'd though it seems.

This breathed itself to life in Julie, *this*
Invested her with all that's wild and sweet ;
This hallow'd, too, the memorable kiss
Which every morn his fever'd lip would greet,
From hers, who but with friendship his would meet ;
But to that gentle touch, through brain and breast
Flash'd the thrill'd spirit's love-devouring heat ;
In that absorbing sigh perchance more blest
Than vulgar minds may be with all they seek possest.
GEORGE, LORD BYRON.

LIV

A MEDITATION FOR HIS MISTRESSE

You are a tulip seen to-day,
But, dearest, of so short a stay
That where you grew, scarce man can say.

You are a lovely July-flower,
Yet one rude wind or ruffling shower
Will force you hence, and in an hour.

You are a sparkling rose i' th' bud,
Yet lost, ere that chaste flesh and blood
Can show where you or grew or stood.

You are a dainty violet,
Yet withered, ere you can be set
Within the virgin's coronet.

You are the queen all flowers among,
But die you must, fair maid, ere long,
As he, the maker of this song.
                          ROBERT HERRICK.

LV

THINGS base and vile, holding no quantity,
Love can transpose to form and dignity.
Love looks not with the eyes, but with the mind ;
And therefore is winged Cupid painted blind.
Nor hath love's mind of any judgment taste ;
Wings and no eyes figure unheedy haste :
And therefore is love said to be a child,
Because in choice he is so oft beguiled.
                          WILLIAM SHAKESPEARE.

LVI

LOVE'S IMMORTALITY

THEY sin who tell us Love can die.
With life all other passions fly,
All others are but vanity.
In Heaven Ambition cannot dwell,

Nor Avarice in the vaults of hell ;
Earthly these passions of the earth,
They perish where they have their birth,
But Love is indestructible.
Its holy flame for ever burneth,
From Heaven it came, to Heaven returneth ;
Too oft on earth a troubled guest,
At times deceived, at times opprest,
It here is tried and purified,
Then hath in Heaven its perfect rest :
It soweth here with toil and care,
But the harvest-time of love is there.

ROBERT SOUTHEY.

LVII

FIE, foolish Earth, think you the heaven wants glory,
Because your shadows do yourself benight ?
All's dark unto the blind, let them be sorry ;
The heavens in themselves are ever bright.

Fie, fond desire, think you that Love wants glory,
Because your shadows do yourself benight ?
The hopes and fears of lust may make men sorry,
But love still in herself finds her delight.

Then Earth stand fast, the sky that you benight
Will turn again, and so restore your glory ;
Desire be steady, hope is your delight,
An orb wherein no creature can be sorry ;
Love being placed above these middle regions,
Where every passion wars itself with legions.

FULKE GREVILLE, LORD BROOKE.

LVIII

THE MARRIED LOVER

WHY, having won her, do I woo?
    Because her spirit's vestal grace
Provokes me always to pursue,
    But, spirit-like, eludes embrace ; ·
Because her womanhood is such
    That, as on court-days subjects kiss
The Queen's hand, yet so near a touch
    Affirms no mean familiarness,
Nay, rather marks more fair the height
    Which can with safety so neglect
To dread, as lower ladies might,
    That grace should meet with disrespect ;
Thus she with happy favour feeds
    Allegiance from a love so high
That thence no false conceit proceeds
    Of difference bridged, or state put by ;
Because, although in act and word
    As lowly as a wife can be,
Her manners, when they call me lord,
    Remind me 'tis by courtesy ;
Not with her least consent of will,
    Which would my proud affection hurt,
But by the noble style that still
    Imputes an unattained desert ;
Because her gay and lofty brows,
    When all is won which hope can ask,
Reflect a light of hopeless snows
    That bright in virgin ether bask ;

Because, though free of the outer court
I am, this Temple keeps its shrine
Sacred to heaven ; because, in short,
She's not and never can be mine.

COVENTRY PATMORE.

LIX

THE joys of Love, if they should ever last,
Without affliction or disquietness,
That worldly chances do among them cast,
Would be on earth too great a blessedness ;
Liker to heaven than mortal wretchedness.
Therefore the winged God, to let men weet
That here on earth is no sure happiness,
A thousand sours hath temper'd with one sweet,
To make it seem more dear and dainty, as is meet.

EDMUND SPENSER.

LX

THE FIRST BRIDAL

(Adam loquitur.)

ABSTRACT as in a trance, methought I saw,
Though sleeping, where I lay, and saw the Shape
Still glorious before whom awake I stood ;
Who, stooping, opened my left side, and took
From thence a rib, with cordial spirits warm,
And life-blood streaming fresh ; wide was the wound,
But suddenly with flesh filled up and healed.
The rib he formed and fashioned with his hands ;
Under his forming hands a creature grew,
Man-like, but different sex, so lovely fair

That what seemed fair in all the world seemed now
Mean, or in her summed up, in her contained
And in her looks, which from that time infused
Sweetness into my heart unfelt before,
And into all things from her air inspired
The spirit of love and amorous delight.
She disappeared, and left me dark; I waked
To find her, or for ever to deplore
Her loss, and other pleasures all abjure :
When, out of hope, behold her not far off,
Such as I saw her in my dream, adorned
With what all Earth or Heaven could bestow
To make her amiable.   On she came,
Led by her Heavenly Maker, though unseen
And guided by His voice, nor uninformed
Of nuptial sanctity and marriage rites.
Grace was in all her steps, heaven in her eye,
In every gesture dignity and love.
I, overjoyed, could not forbear aloud : —
   "This turn hath made amends ; thou hast fulfilled
Thy words, Creator bounteous and benign,
Giver of all things fair—but fairest this
Of all thy gifts !—nor enviest.   I now see
Bone of my bone, flesh of my flesh, my Self
Before me.   Woman is her name, of Man
Extracted ; for this cause he shall forego
Father and mother, and to his wife adhere,
And they shall be one flesh, one heart, one soul."
   She heard me thus ; and, though divinely brought,
Yet innocence and virgin modesty,
Her virtue, and the conscience of her worth,
That would be wooed, and not unsought be won,
Not obvious, not obtrusive, but retired,
The more desirable—or, to say all,
Nature herself, though pure of sinful thought—

Wrought in her so, that, seeing me, she turned.
I followed her ; she what was honour knew,
And with obsequious majesty approved
My pleaded reason.   To the nuptial bower
I led her blushing like the Morn ; all Heaven,
And happy constellations, on that hour
Shed their selectest influence ; the Earth
Gave sign of gratulation, and each hill ;
Joyous the birds ; fresh gales and gentle airs
Whispered it to the woods, and from their wings
Flung rose, flung odours from the spicy shrub,
Disporting, till the amorous bird of night
Sung spousal, and bid haste the Evening-star
On his hill-top to light the bridal lamp.
    Thus have I told thee all my state, and brought
My story to the sum of earthly bliss
Which I enjoy, and must confess to find
In all things else delight indeed, but such
As, used or not, works in the mind no change,
Nor vehement desire—these delicacies
I mean of taste, sight, smell, herbs, fruits, and flowers,
Walks, and the melody of birds : but here,
Far otherwise, transported I behold,
Transported touch ; here passion first I felt,
Commotion strange, in all enjoyments else
Superior and unmoved, here only weak
Against the charm of beauty's powerful glance.
Or Nature failed in me, and left some part
Not proof enough such object to sustain,
Or from my side subducting, took perhaps
More than enough—at least on her bestowed
Too much of ornament, in outward show
Elaborate, of inward less exact.
For well I understand in the prime end
Of Nature her the inferior, in the mind

And inward faculties, which most excel ;
In outward also her resembling less
His image who made both, and less expressing
The character of that dominion given
O'er other creatures.   Yet, when I approach
Her loveliness, so absolute she seems
And in herself complete, so well to know
Her own, that what she wills to do or say
Seems wisest, virtuousest, discreetest, best.
All higher Knowledge in her presence falls
Degraded ; Wisdom in discourse with her
Loses, discountenanced, and like Folly shows ;
Authority and Reason on her wait,
As one intended first, not after made
Occasionally ; and, to consummate all,
Greatness of mind and nobleness their seat
Build in her loveliest, and create an awe
About her, as a guard angelic placed.

                                     JOHN MILTON.

LXI

LOVE'S NOBLENESS

FOR love is Lord of truth and loyalty,
Lifting himself out of the lowly dust
On golden plumes up to the purest sky,
Above the reach of loathly sinful lust,
Whose base affect through cowardly distrust
Of his weak wings dares not to heaven fly,
But like a moldwarp in the earth doth lie.

His dunghill thoughts, which do themselves enure
To dirty dross, no higher dare aspire,
Ne can his feeble earthly eyes endure

The flaming light of that celestial fire
Which kindleth love in generous desire,
And makes him mount above the native might
Of heavy earth, up to the heaven's height.

Such is the power of that sweet passion,
That it all sordid baseness doth expel,
And the refined mind doth newly fashion
Unto a fairer form, which now doth dwell
In his high thought, that would itself excel,
Which he beholding still with constant sight,
Admires the mirror of so heavenly light.

Whose image printing in his deepest wit,
He thereon feeds his hungry fantasy,
Still full, yet never satisfied with it;
Like Tantale that in store doth starvèd lie,
So doth he pine in most satiety;
For nought may quench his infinite desire,
Once kindled through that first conceived fire.

Thereon his mind affixèd wholly is,
Ne thinks on aught but how it to attain;
His care, his joy, his hope, is all on this,
That seems in it all blisses to contain,
In sight whereof all other bliss seems vain:
Thrice happy man! might he the same possess,
He feigns himself, and doth his fortune bless.

And though he do not win his wish to end,
Yet thus far happy he himself doth ween,
That heavens such happy grace did to him lend,
As thing on earth so heavenly to have seen,
His heart's enshrinèd saint, his heaven's queen,
Fairer than fairest, in his feigning eye,
Whose sole aspect he counts felicity.

Then forth he casts in his unquiet thought,
What he may do, her favour to obtain,
What brave exploit, what peril hardly wrought,
What puissant conquest, what adventurous pain,
May please her best, and grace unto him gain ;
He dreads no danger, nor misfortune fears,
His faith, his fortune, in his breast he bears.

Thou art his god, thou art his mighty guide,
Thou, being blind, let'st him not see his fears,
But carriest him to that which he had eyed,
Through seas, through flames, through thousand
    swords and spears ;
Ne ought so strong that may his force withstand,
With which thou armest his resistless hand.
                              EDMUND SPENSER.

LOVE AND NATURE

Now came the Spring, when free-born Love
Calls up nature in forest and grove,
And makes each thing leap forth, and be
Loving, and lovely, and blithe as he.

LEIGH HUNT.

In amorous descant all a summer's day.

MILTON.

LXII

Now sleeps the crimson petal, now the white ;
Nor waves the cypress in the palace walk ;
Nor winks the gold fin in the porphyry font :
The firefly wakens : waken thou with me.

Now droops the milkwhite peacock like a ghost,
And like a ghost she glimmers on to me.

Now lies the Earth all Danaë to the stars,
And all thy heart lies open unto me.

Now slides the silent meteor on, and leaves
A shining furrow, as thy thoughts in me.

Now folds the lily all her sweetness up,
And slips into the bosom of the lake ;
So fold thyself, my dearest, thou, and slip
Into my bosom and be lost in me.

ALFRED, LORD TENNYSON.

LXIII

SWEET FA'S THE EVE

SWEET fa's the eve on Craigie-burn,
    And blythe awakes the morrow,
But a' the pride o' spring's return
    Can yield me nocht but sorrow.

II

I see the flowers and spreading trees,
 I hear the wild birds singing;
But what a weary wight can please,
 And care his bosom wringing?

Fain, fain would I my griefs impart,
 Yet dare na for your anger;
But secret love will break my heart,
 If I conceal it langer.

If thou refuse to pity me,
 If thou shalt love anither,
When yon green leaves fa' frae the tree,
 Around my grave they'll wither.

       ROBERT BURNS.

LXIV

HAVE you seen but a bright lily grow
 Before rude hands have touch'd it?
Have you mark'd but the fall of the snow
 Before the soil hath smutch'd it?
Have you felt the wool of the beaver?
 Or swan's down ever?
Or have smelt o' the bud of the briar?
 Or the nard in the fire?
Or have tasted the bag of the bee?
 O, so white! O, so soft! O, so sweet is she!

       BEN JONSON.

LXV

SING HEIGH-HO !

THERE sits a bird on every tree ;
    Sing heigh-ho !
There sits a bird on every tree,
And courts his love as I do thee ;
    Sing heigh-ho, and heigh-ho !
  Young maids must marry.

There grows a flower on every bough ;
    Sing heigh-ho !
There grows a flower on every bough,
Its petals kiss—I'll show you how :
    Sing heigh-ho, and heigh-ho !
  Young maids must marry.

From sea to stream the salmon roam ;
    Sing heigh-ho !
From sea to stream the salmon roam ;
Each finds a mate and leads her home ;
    Sing heigh-ho, and heigh-ho !
  Young maids must marry.

The sun's a bridegroom, earth a bride ;
    Sing heigh-ho !
They court from morn till eventide :
The earth shall pass, but love abide.
    Sing heigh-ho, and heigh-ho !
  Young maids must marry.
            CHARLES KINGSLEY.

LXVI

HARK! THE MAVIS

CHORUS.

CA' the yowes to the knowes,
Ca' them where the heather grows,
Ca' them where the burnie rows,
    My bonny dearie.

Hark! the mavis' evening sang
Sounding Clouden's woods amang,
Then a-faulding let us gang,
    My bonny dearie.
        Ca' the, etc.

We'll gae down by Clouden side,
Through the hazels spreading wide,
O'er the waves that sweetly glide,
    To the moon sae clearly.
        Ca' the, etc.

Yonder Clouden's silent towers,
Where at moonshine midnight hours,
O'er the dewy bending flowers,
    Fairies dance sae cheery.
        Ca' the, etc.

Ghaist nor bogle shalt thou fear;
Thou'rt to love and Heaven sae dear,
Nocht of ill may come thee near,
    My bonny dearie.
        Ca' the, etc.

Fair and lovely as thou art,
Thou hast stown my very heart ;
I can die—but canna part,
  My bonny dearie.
     Ca' the, etc.

While waters wimple to the sea ;
While day blinks in the lift sae hie ;
Till clay-cauld death shall blin' my e'e
  Ye shall be my dearie.
     Ca' the, etc.

ROBERT BURNS.

LXVII

LOVE'S LIKENESS

O, MARK yon Rose-tree ! when the West
Breathes on her with too warm a zest,
  She turns her cheek away,
Yet, if one moment he refrain,
She turns her cheek to him again,
  And wooes him still to stay.

Is she not like a maiden coy
Pressed by some amorous-breathing boy?
  Though coy, she courts him too :
Winding away her slender form,
She will not have him woo so warm,
  And yet will have him woo !

GEORGE DARLEY.

LXVIII

O SWALLOW, Swallow, flying, flying South,
Fly to her, and fall upon her gilded eaves,
And tell her, tell her, what I tell to thee.

O tell her, Swallow, that thou knowest each,
That bright and fierce and fickle is the South,
And dark and true and tender is the North.

O Swallow, Swallow, if I could follow, and light
Upon her lattice, I would pipe and trill,
And cheep and twitter twenty million loves.

O were I thou that she might take me in,
And lay me on her bosom, and her heart
Would rock the snowy cradle till I died.

Why lingereth she to clothe her heart with love,
Delaying as the tender ash delays
To clothe herself, when all the woods are green?

O tell her, Swallow, that thy brood is flown:
Say to her, I do but wanton in the South,
But in the North long since my nest is made.

O tell her, brief is life, but love is long,
And brief the sun of summer in the North,
And brief the moon of beauty in the South.

O Swallow, flying from the golden woods,
Fly to her, and pipe and woo her, and make her mine,
And tell her, tell her, that I follow thee.

ALFRED, LORD TENNYSON.

LXIX

A SLUMBER did my spirit seal ;
  I had no human fears :
She seem'd a thing that could not feel
  The touch of earthly years.

No motion has she now, no force ;
  She neither hears nor sees ;
Roll'd round in earth's diurnal course
  With rocks, and stones, and trees.
              WILLIAM WORDSWORTH.

LXX

THE bee to the heather,
  The lark to the sky,
The roe to the greenwood,
  And whither shall I ?

Oh, Alice ! ah, Alice !
  So sweet to the bee
Are the moorland and heather
  By Cannock and Leigh !

Oh, Alice ! ah, Alice !
  O'er Teddesley Park
The sunny sky scatters
  The notes of the lark !

Oh, Alice ! ah, Alice !
  In Beaudesert glade
The roes toss their antlers
  For joy of the shade !—

But Alice, dear Alice !
  Glade, moorland, nor sky
Without you can content me,
  And whither shall I ?
                    SIR HENRY TAYLOR.

LXXI

WHERE, upon Apennine slope, with the chestnut the oak-
    trees immingle,
  Where, amid odorous copse, bridle-paths wander and
      wind,
Where, under mulberry branches, the diligent rivulet
    sparkles,
  Or, amid cotton and maize, peasants their water-works
      ply,
Where, over fig-tree and orange in tier upon tier still re-
    peated,
  Garden on garden upreared, balconies step to the sky,—
Ah, that I were far away from the crowd and the streets
    of the city,
  Under the vine-trellis laid, O my belovèd, with thee !
                    ARTHUR HUGH CLOUGH.

LXXII

A SONG OF THE FOUR SEASONS

  WHEN Spring comes laughing
    By vale and hill,
  By wind-flower walking
    And daffodil,—

Sing stars of morning,
  Sing morning skies,
Sing blue of speedwell,—
  And my Love's eyes.

When comes the Summer
  Full-leaved and strong,
And gay birds gossip
  The orchard long,—
Sing hid, sweet honey
  That no bee sips ;
Sing red, red roses,—
  And my Love's lips.

When Autumn scatters
  The leaves again,
And piled sheaves bury
  The broad-wheeled wain,—
Sing flutes of harvest
  Where men rejoice ;
Sing rounds of reapers,—
  And my Love's voice.

But when comes Winter
  With hail and storm,
And red fire roaring
  And ingle warm,—
Sing first sad going
  Of friends that part :
Then sing glad meeting,—
  And my Love's heart.

AUSTIN DOBSON.

LXXIII

LOVE'S GOOD-MORROW

PACK clouds away, and welcome day,
  With night we banish sorrow;
Sweet air blow soft, larks mount aloft,
  To give my love good-morrow.
Wings from the wind to please her mind,
  Notes from the lark I'll borrow;
Bird prune thy wing, nightingale sing,
  To give my love good-morrow,
  Notes from them both I'll borrow.

Wake from thy nest, robin-red-breast,
  Sing birds in every furrow;
And from each hill let music shrill
  Give my fair love good-morrow.
Blackbird, and thrush, in every bush,
  Stare, linnet, and cock-sparrow!
You pretty elves, among yourselves,
  Sing my fair love good-morrow.
  To give my love good-morrow,
  Sing birds in every furrow.
                          THOMAS HEYWOOD.

LXXIV

THE SAILOR'S RETURN

HIGH over the breakers,
Low under the lee,
Sing ho
The billow,
And the lash of the rolling sea!

Boat, boat, to the billow,
Boat, boat to the lee !
Love, on thy pillow,
Art thou dreaming of me ?

Billow, billow, breaking,
Land us low on the lee !
For sleeping or waking,
Sweet love, I am coming to thee !

High, high, o'er the breakers,
Low, low, on the lee, .
Sing ho !
The billow
That brings me back to thee !

SYDNEY DOBELL.

LXXV

THE BIRKS OF ABERFELDY

CHORUS.

BONNY lassie, will ye go, will ye go, will ye go,
Bonny lassie, will ye go to the Birks of Aberfeldy?

Now simmer blinks on flowery braes,
And o'er the crystal streamlet plays,
Come let us spend the lightsome days
  In the Birks of Aberfeldy.
    Bonny lassie, etc.

While o'er their heads the hazels hing,
The little birdies blythly sing,
Or lightly flit on wanton wing
  In the Birks of Aberfeldy.
    Bonny lassie, etc.

The braes ascend like lofty wa's,
The foaming stream deep roaring fa's,
O'erhung wi' fragrant spreading shaws,
   The Birks of Aberfeldy.
      Bonny lassie, etc.

The hoary cliffs are crown'd wi' flowers,
White o'er the linns the burnie pours,
And rising, weets wi' misty showers
   The Birks of Aberfeldy.
      Bonny lassie, etc.

Let fortune's gifts at random flee,
They ne'er shall draw a wish frae me,
Supremely blest wi' love and thee
   In the Birks of Aberfeldy.
      Bonny lassie, etc.

ROBERT BURNS.

LXXVI

LOVE within the lover's breast
Burns like Hesper in the West,
O'er the ashes of the sun,
Till the day and night are done;
Then, when dawn drives up his car—
Lo! it is the morning star.

Love! thy love pours down on mine,
As the sunlight on the vine,
As the snow rill on the vale,
As the salt breeze on the sail;
As the song unto the bird
On my lips thy name is heard.

As a dewdrop on the rose
In thy heart my passion glows ;
As a skylark to the sky,
Up into thy breast I fly ;
As a sea-shell of the sea
Ever shall I sing of thee.

GEORGE MEREDITH.

LXXVII

THE nightingale has a lyre of gold,
    The lark's is a clarion call,
And the blackbird plays but a boxwood flute,
    But I love him best of all.

For his song is all of the joy of life,
    And we in the mad spring weather,
We too have listened till he sang
    Our hearts and lips together.

WILLIAM ERNEST HENLEY.

LXXVIII

CLAUD HALCRO'S SONG

FAREWELL to Northmaven,
    Gray Hillswicke, farewell !
To the calms of thy haven,
    The storms on thy fell—
To each breeze that can vary
    The mood of thy main,
And to thee, bonny Mary !
    We meet not again.

Farewell the wild ferry,
   Which Hacon could brave,
When the peaks of the Skerry
   Where white in the wave.
There's a maid may look over
   These wild waves in vain,
For the skiff of her lover—
   He comes not again.

The vows thou hast broke,
   On the wild currents fling them ;
On the quicksand and rock
   Let the mermaiden sing them.
New sweetness they'll give her
   Bewildering strain ;
But there's one who will never
   Believe them again.

O were there an island,
   Though ever so wild,
Where woman could smile, and
   No man be beguiled—
Too tempting a snare
   To poor mortals were given ;
And the hope would fix there,
   That should anchor on heaven.
            SIR WALTER SCOTT.

LXXIX

THE LASSIE I LO'E BEST

OF a' the airts the wind can blaw,
   I dearly like the west,
For there the bonny lassie lives,
   The lassie I lo'e best :

There wild woods grow, and rivers row,
  And mony a hill between ;
But day and night my fancy's flight
  Is ever wi' my Jean.

I see her in the dewy flowers,
  I see her sweet and fair :
I hear her in the tunefu' birds,
  I hear her charm the air :
There's not a bonny flower that springs
  By fountain, shaw, or green,
There's not a bonny birdie sings,
  But minds me o' my Jean.
                    ROBERT BURNS.

LXXX

O WEEL befa' the guileless heart
  In cottage, bught, or pen !
And weel befa' the bonny May
  That wons in yonder glen ;
Wha lo'es the good and true sae weel—
Wha's aye sae kind and aye sae leal,
And pure as blooming asphodel
  Amang sae mony men ;
O weel befa' the bonnie thing
  That wons in yonder glen.

'Tis sweet to hear the music float
  Alang the gloaming lea ;
'Tis sweet to hear the blackbird's note
  Come pealing frae the tree ;
To see the lambkin's lightsome race ;
The speckled kid in wanton chase ;

The young deer cower in lonely place
   Deep in his flowery den ;
But what is like the bonnie face
   That smiles in yonder glen ?

There's beauty in the violet's vest,
   There's hinny in the haw,
There's dew within the rose's breast,
   The sweetest o' them a'.
The sun may rise and set again,
And lace wi' burning gowd the main,
The rainbow bend out ow're the plain
   Sae lovely to the ken ;
But there's naething like my bonnie thing
   That wons in yonder glen.

JAMES HOGG.

LXXXI

HARK ! hark ! the lark at heaven's gate sings,
   And Phœbus 'gins arise,
His steeds to water at those springs
   On chaliced flowers that lies ;
And winking Mary-buds begin
   To ope their golden eyes :
With everything that pretty bin,
   My lady sweet, arise ;
     Arise, arise.

WILLIAM SHAKESPEARE.

LXXXII

SHE dwelt among the untrodden ways
   Beside the springs of Dove ;
A maid whom there were few to praise,
   And very few to love.

A violet by a mossy stone
　Half-hidden from the eye !
Fair as a star, when only one
　Is shining in the sky.

She lived unknown, and few could know
　When Lucy ceased 'to be ;
But she is in her grave, and, oh,
　_The difference to me !

WILLIAM WORDSWORTH.

LXXXIII

THE WOODLARK

O STAY, sweet warbling woodlark, stay,
Nor quit for me the trembling spray :
A hapless lover courts thy lay,
　Thy soothing, fond complaining.

Again, again that tender part,
That I may catch thy melting art !
For surely that wad touch her heart,
　Wha kills me wi' disdaining.

Say, was thy little mate unkind,
And heard thee as the careless wind ?
Oh, nocht but love and sorrow joined
　Sic notes o' wae could wauken.

Thou tells o' never-ending care,
O' speechless grief and dark despair ;
For pity's sake, sweet bird, nae mair !
　Or my poor heart is broken.

ROBERT BURNS.

LXXXIV

A WILD ROSE

THE first wild rose in wayside hedge,
   This year I wandering see,
I pluck, and send it as a pledge,
   My own Wild Rose, to thee.

For when my gaze first met thy gaze,
   We were knee-deep in June :
The nights were only dreamier days,
   And all the hours in tune.

I found thee, like the eglantine,
   Sweet, simple, and apart ;
And, from that hour, thy smile hath been
   The flower that scents my heart.

And, ever since, when tendrils grace
   Young copse or weathered bole
With rosebuds, straight I see thy face,
   And gaze into thy soul.

A natural bud of love thou art,
   Where, gazing down, I view,
Deep hidden in thy fragrant heart,
   A drop of heavenly dew.

Go, wild rose, to my Wild Rose dear ;
   Bid her come swift and soon.
O would that She were always here !
   It then were always June.

               ALFRED AUSTIN.

LXXXV

WHEN THE KYE COMES HAME

COME all ye jolly shepherds
  That whistle through the glen,
I'll tell ye of a secret
  That courtiers dinna ken :
What is the greatest bliss
  That the tongue o' man can name?
'Tis to woo a bonny lassie
  When the kye comes hame.
     When the kye comes hame,
     When the kye comes hame,
    'Tween the gloaming and the mirk
     When the kye comes hame.

'Tis not beneath the coronet,
  Nor canopy of state,
'Tis not on couch of velvet,
  Nor arbour of the great—
'Tis beneath the spreading birk,
  In the glen without the name,
Wi' a bonny, bonny lassie
  When the kye comes hame.
     When the kye comes hame, etc.

There the blackbird bigs his nest
  For the mate he loes to see,
And on the topmost bough,
  O, a happy bird is he ;
Where he pours his melting ditty
  And love is a' the theme,
And he'll woo his bonny lassie
  When the kye comes hame.
     When the kye comes hame, etc.

When the blewart bears a pearl,
 And the daisy turns a pea,
And the bonny lucken gowan
 Has fauldit up her ee,
Then the laverock frae the blue lift
 Drops down, an' thinks nae shame
To woo his bonny lassie
 When the kye comes hame.
   When the kye comes hame, etc.

See yonder pawkie shepherd,
 That lingers on the hill,
His ewes are in the fauld,
 - An' his lambs are lying still;
Yet he downa gang to bed,
 For his heart is in a flame,
To meet his bonny lassie
 When the kye comes hame.
   When the kye comes hame, etc.

When the little wee bit heart
 Rises high in the breast,
An' the little wee bit starn
 Rises red in the east,
O there's a joy sae dear,
 That the heart can hardly frame,
Wi' a bonny, bonny lassie
 When the kye comes hame.
   When the kye comes hame, etc.

Then since all nature joins
 In this love without alloy,
O, wha would prove a traitor
 To Nature's dearest joy?
Or wha would choose a crown,
 Wi' its perils and its fame,

And *miss* his bonny lassie
    When the kye comes hame?
      When the kye comes hame,
      When the kye comes hame,
    'Tween the gloaming and the mirk
      When the kye comes home.

JAMES HOGG.

LXXXVI

DUET

(IN ROSAMUND'S BOWER)

1. Is it the wind of the dawn that I hear in the pine overhead?

2. No; but the voice of the deep as it hollows the cliffs of the land.

1. Is there a voice coming up with the voice of the deep from the strand,
  One coming up with a song in the flush of the glimmering red?

2. Love that is born of the deep coming up with the sun from the sea.

1. Love that can shape or can shatter a life till the life shall have fled?

2. Nay, let us welcome him, Love that can lift up a life from the dead.

1. Keep him away from the lone little isle. Let us be, let us be.

2. Nay, let him make it his own, let him reign in it—he, it is he,
  Love that is born of the deep coming up with the sun from the sea.

ALFRED, LORD TENNYSON.

LXXXVII

TO ——

MUSIC, when soft voices die,
Vibrates in the memory ;
Odours, when sweet violets sicken,
Live within the sense they quicken ;

Rose leaves, when the rose is dead,
Are heaped for the belovèd's bed ;
And so thy thoughts, when thou art gone,
Love itself shall slumber on.

PERCY BYSSHE SHELLEY.

LXXXVIII

THE POSIE

O LUVE will venture in, where it daur na weel be seen,
O luve will venture in, where wisdom ance has been ;
But I will down yon river rove, amang the wood sae
    green,
    And a' to pu' a Posie to my ain dear May.

The primrose I will pu', the firstling o' the year,
And I will pu' the pink, the emblem o' my dear,
For she's the pink o' womankind, and blooms without a
    peer ;
    And a' to be a Posie to my ain dear May.

I'll pu' the budding rose, when Phœbus peeps in view,
For it's like a baumy kiss o' her sweet, bonny mou ;
The hyacinth's for constancy, wi' its unchanging blue,
    And a' to be a Posie to my ain dear May.

The lily it is pure, and the lily it is fair,
And in her lovely bosom I'll place the lily there ;
The daisy's for simplicity and unaffected air,
  And a' to be a Posie to my ain dear May.

The hawthorn I will pu', wi' its locks o' siller gray,
Where, like an aged man, it stands at break o' day,
But the songster's nest within the bush I winna tak'
    away ;
  And a' to be a Posie to my ain dear May.

The woodbine I will pu' when the e'ening star is near,
And the diamond drops o' dew shall be her een sae
    clear ;
The violet's for modesty which weel she fa's to wear,
  And a' to be a Posie to my ain dear May.

I'll tie the Posie round wi' the silken band o' luve,
And I'll place it in her breast, and I'll swear, by a' above,
That to my latest draught o' life the band shall ne'er
    remove,
  And this will be a Posie to my ain dear May.
                                    ROBERT BURNS.

LXXXIX

THE LOVER'S SONG

When Winter hoar no longer holds
    The young year in his gripe,
And bleating voices fill the folds,
    And blackbirds pair and pipe ;
Then coax the maiden where the sap
    Awakes the woodlands drear,
And pour sweet wildflowers in her lap,
    And sweet words in her ear.

For Springtime is the season, sure,
  Since Love's game first was played,
When tender thoughts begin to lure
  The heart of April maid,
             Of maid,
  The heart of April maid.

When June is wreathed with wilding rose,
  And all the buds are blown,
And O, 'tis joy to dream and doze
  In meadows newly mown ;
Then take her where the graylings leap,
  And where the dabchick dives,
Or where the bees in clover reap
  The harvest for their hives.
For Summer is the season when,
  If you but know the way,
A maid that's kissed will kiss again,
  Then pelt you with the hay,
             The hay,
  Then pelt you with the hay.

When sickles ply among the wheat,
  Then trundle home the sheaves,
And there's a rustling of the feet
  Through early-fallen leaves ;
Entice her where the orchard glows
  With apples plump and tart,
And tell her plain the thing she knows,
  And ask her for her heart.
For Autumn is the season, boy,
  To gather what we sow :
If you be bold, she won't be coy,
  Nor ever say you no,
             Say no,
  Nor ever say you no.

When woodmen clear the coppice lands,
  And arch the hornbeam drive,
And stamp their feet, and chafe their hands,
  To keep their blood alive ;
Then lead her where, when vows are heard,
  The church-bells peal and swing,
And, as the parson speaks the word,
  Then on her clap the ring.
For Winter is a cheerless time
  To live and lie alone ;
But what to him is snow or rime,
  Who calls his love his own,
          His own,
   Who call his love his own ?
         ALFRED AUSTIN.

XC

THE castled crag of Drachenfels
Frowns o'er the wide and winding Rhine,
Whose breast of waters broadly swells
Between the banks which bear the vine,
And hills all rich with blossom'd trees,
And fields which promise corn and wine,
And scatter'd cities crowning these,
Whose far white walls along them shine,
Have strew'd a scene, which I should see
With double joy wert *thou* with me.

And peasant girls, with deep blue eyes,
And hands which offer early flowers,
Walk smiling o'er this paradise ;
Above, the frequent feudal towers

Through green leaves lift their walls of gray,
And many a rock which steeply lowers,
And noble arch in proud decay,
Look o'er this vale of vintage-bowers ;
But one thing want these banks of Rhine—
Thy gentle hand to clasp in mine !

I send the lilies given to me ;
Though long before thy hand they touch,
I know that they must wither'd be,
But yet reject them not as such ;
For I have cherish'd them as dear,
Because they yet may meet thine eye,
And guide thy soul to mine ev'n here,
When thou behold'st them drooping nigh,
And know'st them gather'd by the Rhine,
And offer'd from my heart to thine !

The river nobly foams and flows,
The charm of this enchanted ground,
And all its thousand turns disclose
Some fresher beauty varying round :
The haughtiest breast its wish might bound
Through life to dwell delighted here ;
Nor could on earth a spot be found
To nature and to me so dear,
Could thy dear eyes in following mine
Still sweeten more these banks of Rhine !

GEORGE, LORD BYRON.

XCI

HYMENEAL SONG

ROSES, their sharp spines being gone,
Not royal in their smells alone,
    But in their hue ;
Maiden pinks, of odour faint,
Daisies smell-less, yet most quaint,
    And sweet thyme true ;

Primrose, first-born child of Ver,
Merry spring-time's harbinger,
    With her bells dim ;
Oxlips in their cradles growing,
Marigolds on death-beds blowing,
    Larks'-heels trim ;

All dear Nature's children sweet,
Lie 'fore bride and bridegroom's feet,
    Blessing their sense ! .
Not an angel of the air,
Bird melodious or bird fair,
    Be absent hence !

The crow, the slanderous cuckoo, nor
The boding raven, nor chough hoar,
    Nor chattering pie,
May on our bride-house perch or sing,
Or with them any discord bring,
    But from it fly !
                    WILLIAM SHAKESPEARE.

CHIVALRIC LOVE

Love rules the camp, the court, the grove,
For love is heaven, and heaven is love.

SCOTT.

I vow'd unvarying faith, and she
  To whom in full I pay that vow,
Rewards me with variety
  Which men who change can never know.

COVENTRY PATMORE.

XCII

TO ALTHEA

FROM PRISON

WHEN love with unconfined wings
  Hovers within my gates,
And my divine Althea brings
  To whisper at the grates ;
When I lie tangled in her hair
  And fettered to her eye,
The gods that wanton in the air
  Know no such liberty.

When flowing cups run swiftly round,
  With no allaying Thames,
Our careless heads with roses bound,
  Our hearts with loyal flames ;
When thirsty grief in wine we steep,
  When healths and draughts go free,
Fishes that tipple in the deep
  Know no such liberty.

When, like committed linnets, I
  With shriller throat shall sing
The sweetness, mercy, majesty,
  And glories of my king ;

When I shall voice aloud, how good
    He is, how great should be,
Enlarged winds that curl the flood
    Know no such liberty.

Stone walls do not a prison make,
    Nor iron bars a cage;
Minds innocent and quiet take
    That for an hermitage.
If I have freedom in my love,
    And in my soul am free,
Angels alone that soar above
    Enjoy such liberty.
                  RICHARD LOVELACE.

XCIII

SUCH ones ill judge of Love that cannot love,
Ne in their frozen hearts feel kindly flame:
For-thy they ought not thing unknown reprove,
Ne natural affection faultless blame,
For fault of few that have abused the same;
For it of honour and all virtue is
The root, and brings forth glorious flowers of fame,
That crown true lovers with immortal bliss,
The meed of them that love, and do not live amiss.
                  EDMUND SPENSER.

XCIV

BECAUSE I breathe not love to every one,
Nor do not use set colours for to wear,
Nor nourish special locks of vowèd hair,
Nor give each speech a full point of a groan,

The courtly nymphs, acquainted with the moan
Of them which in their lips Love's standard bear,—
" What, he !" they say of me, "now I dare swear
He cannot love ; no, no, let him alone."
And think so still, so Stella know my mind ;
Profess indeed I do not Cupid's art ;
But you, fair maids, at length this true shall find,
That his right badge is but worn in the heart :
Dumb swans, not chattering pies, do lovers prove ;
They love indeed who quake to say they love.

SIR PHILIP SIDNEY.

XCV

SEEK not the tree of silkiest bark
    And balmiest bud,
To carve her name while yet 'tis dark
    Upon the wood.
The world is full of noble tasks,
    And wreaths hard won :
Each work demands strong hearts, strong hands,
    Till day is done.

Sing not that violet-veinèd skin,
    That cheek's pale roses,
The lily of that form wherein
    Her soul reposes :
Forth to the fight, true man, true knight ;
    The clash of arms
Shall more prevail than whispered tale
    To win her charms.

The warrior for the True, the Right,
    Fights in Love's name :

The love that lures thee from that fight
    Lures thee to shame :
The love which lifts the heart, yet leaves
    The spirit free,
That love, or none, is fit for one
    Man-shaped, like thee.
                   AUBREY DE VERE.

XCVI

TO ANTHEA, WHO MAY COMMAND HIM ANYTHING

BID me to live, and I will live
    Thy Protestant to be :
Or bid me love, and I will give
    A loving heart to thee.

A heart as soft, a heart as kind,
    A heart as sound and free,
As in the whole world thou canst find,
    That heart I'll give to thee.

Bid that heart stay, and it will stay,
    To honour thy decree :
Or bid it languish quite away,
    And 't shalt do so for thee.

Bid me to weep, and I will weep,
    While I have eyes to see :
And having none, yet I will keep
    A heart to weep for thee.

Bid me despair, and I'll despair,
    Under that cypress tree :
Or bid me die, and I will dare
    Ev'n death, to die for thee.

Thou art my life, my love, my heart,   .
   The very eyes of me :
And hast command of every part,
   To live and die for thee.
ROBERT HERRICK.

XCVII

FORGET not yet the tried intent
Of such a truth as I have meant ;
My great travail so gladly spent,
        Forget not yet !

Forget not yet when first began
The weary life ye know, since whan
The suit, the service none tell can ;
        Forget not yet !

Forget not yet the great assays,
The cruel wrong, the scornful ways,
The painful patience in delays,
        Forget not yet !

Forget not ! O, forget not this,
How long ago hath been, and is
The mind that never meant amiss—
        Forget not yet !

Forget not then thine own approved
The which so long hath thee so loved,
Whose steadfast faith yet never moved—
        Forget not this !
SIR THOMAS WYATT.

XCVIII

Fate ! I have asked few things of thee,
    And fewer have to ask.
Shortly, thou knowest, I shall be
    No more : then con thy task.

If one be left on earth so late
    Whose love is like the past,
Tell her in whispers, gentle Fate !
    Not even love must last.

Tell her I leave the noisy feast
    Of life, a little tired,
Amid its pleasures few possessed
    And many undesired.

Tell her with steady pace to come
    And, where my laurels lie,
To throw the freshest on the tomb,
    When it has caught her sigh.

Tell her to stand some steps apart
    From others on that day,
And check the tear (if tear should start)
    Too precious for dull clay.
                 Walter Savage Landor.

XCIX

Having this day my horse, my hand, my lance
Guided so well that I obtained the prize,
Both by the judgment of the English eyes
And of some sent from that sweet enemy France ;

Horsemen my skill in horsemanship advance,
Town folks my strength ; a daintier judge applies
His praise to sleight which from good use doth rise ;
Some lucky wits impute it but to chance ;
Others, because of both sides I do take
My blood from them who did excel in this,
Think Nature me a man-at-arms did make.
How far they shot awry ! the true cause is,
Stella look'd on, and from her heavenly face
Sent forth the beams which made so fair my race.

SIR PHILIP SIDNEY.

C

Joy of my life ! full oft for loving you
I bless my lot, that was so lucky placed :
But then the more your own mishap I rue,
That are so much by so mean love embased.
For, had the equal heavens so much you graced
In this as in the rest, ye mote invent
Some heavenly wit, whose verse could have enchased
Your glorious name in golden monument.
But since ye deigned so goodly to relent
To me your thrall, in whom is little worth ;
That little, that I am, shall all be spent
In setting your immortal praises forth :
Whose lofty argument, uplifting me,
Shall lift you up unto an high degree.

EDMUND SPENSER.

CI

IF doughty deeds my lady please,
  Right soon I'll mount my steed ;
And strong his arm, and fast his seat
  That bears frae me the meed.
I'll wear thy colours in my cap,
  Thy picture at my heart ;
And he that bends not to thine eye
  Shall rue it to his smart !
      Then tell me how to woo thee, Love ;
        O tell me how to woo thee !
      For thy dear sake, nae care I'll take
        Tho' ne'er another trow me.

If gay attire delight thine eye,
  I'll dight me in array ;
I'll tend thy chamber door all night,
  And squire thee all the day.
If sweetest sounds can win thine ear,
  These sounds I'll strive to catch ;
Thy voice I'll steal to woo thysell,
  That voice that none can match.

But if fond love thy heart can gain,
  I never broke a vow :
Nae maiden lays her skaith to me,
  I never loved but you.
For you alone I ride the ring,
  For you I wear the blue ;
For you alone I strive to sing,
  O tell me how to woo !
      Then tell me how to woo thee, Love ;
        O tell me how to woo thee !
      For thy dear sake, nae care I'll take,
        Tho' ne'er another trow me !

GRAHAM OF GARTMORE.

CII

TO ——

'I FEAR thy kisses, gentle maiden,
    Thou needest not fear mine ;
My spirit is too deeply laden
    Ever to burthen thine.

I fear thy mien, thy tones, thy motion,
    Thou needest not fear mine ;
Innocent is the heart's devotion
    With which I worship thine.
            PERCY BYSSHE SHELLEY.

CIII

WONDER it is to see, in divers minds,
How diversely love doth his pageants play,
And shows his power in variable kinds :
The baser wit, whose idle thoughts alway
Are wont to cleave unto the lowly clay,
It stirreth up to sensual desire,
And in lewd sloth to waste his careless day ;
But in brave spirit it kindles goodly fire,
That to all high desert and honour doth aspire.
            EDMUND SPENSER.

CIV

SONG TO AMORET

If I were dead, and in my place
  Some fresher youth design'd,
To warm thee with new fires, and grace
  Those arms I left behind;

Were he as faithful as the sun
  That's wedded to the sphere,
His blood as chaste and temperate run
  As April's mildest tear;

Or were he rich, and with his heap
  And spacious share of earth
Could make divine affection cheap
  And court his golden birth;

For all these arts I'd not believe
  (No, though he should be thine)
The mighty Amorist could give
  So rich a heart as mine.

Fortune and beauty thou might'st find,
  And greater men than I;
But my true resolvèd mind
  They never shall come nigh.

For I not for an hour did love,
  Or for a day desire,
But with my soul had from above
  This endless holy fire.

                              HENRY VAUGHAN.

CV

SONG

DRINK ye to her that each loves best,
    And if you nurse a flame
That's told but to her mutual breast,
    We will not ask her name.

Enough, while memory tranced and glad
    Paints silently the fair,
That each should dream of joys he's had,
    Or yet may hope to share.

Yet far, far hence be jest or boast
    From hallow'd thoughts so dear ;
But drink to her that each loves most,
    As she would love to hear.
                THOMAS CAMPBELL.

CVI

BRIGHT star of beauty, on whose eyelids sit
A thousand nymph-like and enamoured graces,
The goddesses of memory and wit,
Which there in order take their several places,
In whose dear bosom sweet delicious Love
Lays down his quiver which he once did bear,
Since he that blessed paradise did prove,
And leaves his mother's lap to sport him there ;
Let others strive to entertain with words,—
My soul is of a braver metal made ;
I hold that vile, which vulgar wit affords ;
In me's that faith which time can not invade.
Let what I praise be still made good by you :
Be you most worthy, whilst I am most true.
                MICHAEL DRAYTON.

CVII

SONG

WHAT care I though beauty fading,
  Die ere time can turn his glass,
What though locks the Graces braiding,
  Perish like the summer grass?
Though thy charms should all decay,
Think not my affections may.

For thy charms, though bright as morning,
  Captured not my idle heart;
Love so grounded ends in scorning,
  Lacks the barb to hold the dart.
My devotion more secure
Wooes thy spirit high and pure.
            WILLIAM CALDWELL ROSCOE.

CVIII

MONTROSE'S LOVE

MY dear and only love, I pray
  That little world of thee
Be governed by no other sway
  But purest monarchy;
For if confusion have a part,
  Which virtuous souls abhor,
And hold a synod in my heart,
  I'll never love thee more.

Like Alexander I will reign,
  And I will reign alone:
My thoughts did evermore disdain
  A rival on my throne.

He either fears his fate too much,
  Or his deserts are small,
Who dares not put it to the touch,
  To gain or lose it all.

But if thou wilt prove faithful then,
  And constant of thy word,
I'll make thee glorious by my pen,
  And famous by my sword.
I'll serve thee in such noble ways
  Was never heard before ;
I'll crown and deck thee all with bays,
  And love thee more and more.
     JAMES GRAHAM, MARQUIS OF MONTROSE.

CIX

TELL me not, sweet, I am unkind,
  That from the nunnery
Of thy chaste breast and quiet mind
  To war and arms I fly.

True, a new mistress now I chase,
  The first foe in the field,
And with a stronger faith embrace
  A sword, a horse, a shield.

Yet this inconstancy is such
  As you too shall adore ;
I could not love thee, dear, so much,
  Loved I not Honour more.
     RICHARD LOVELACE.

LOVE'S DIVINE COMEDY

A lover may bestride the gossamer
That idles in the wanton summer air,
And yet not fall.

SHAKESPEARE.

Love in these labyrinths his slaves detains,
And mighty hearts are held in slender chains.

POPE.

Love's the noblest frailty of the mind.

DRYDEN.

THOU know'st the mask of night is on my face,
Else would a maiden blush bepaint my cheek
For that which thou hast heard me speak to-night.
Fain would I dwell on form, fain, fain deny
What I have spoke : but farewell compliment !
Dost thou love me ?   I know thou wilt say " Ay,"
And I will take thy word : yet, if thou swear'st,
Thou mayst prove false ; at lovers' perjuries,
They say, Jove laughs.   O gentle Romeo,
If thou dost love, pronounce it faithfully :
Or if thou think'st I am too quickly won,
I'll frown and be perverse, and say thee nay,
So thou wilt woo ; but else, not for the world.
In truth, fair Montague, I am too fond,
And therefore thou mayst think my 'haviour light :
But trust me, gentleman, I'll prove more true
Than those that have more cunning to be strange.
I should have been more strange, I must confess,
But that thou overheard'st, ere I was 'ware,
My true love's passion : therefore pardon me,
And not impute this yielding to light love,
Which the dark night hath so discovered.

WILLIAM SHAKESPEARE.

CXI

IT is the miller's daughter,
  And she is grown so dear, so dear,
That I would be the jewel
  That trembles in her ear :
For hid in ringlets day and night,
I'd touch her neck so warm and white.

And I would be the girdle
  About her dainty dainty waist,
And her heart would beat against me,
  In sorrow and in rest ;
And I should know if it beat right,
I'd clasp it round so close and tight.

And I would be the necklace,
  And all day long to fall and rise
Upon her balmy bosom,
  With her laughter or her sighs,
And I would lie so light, so light,
I scarce should be unclasp'd at night.

ALFRED, LORD TENNYSON.

CXII

AT HER WINDOW

BEATING heart ! we come again
  Where my Love reposes :
This is Mabel's window-pane ;
  These are Mabel's roses.

Is she nested? Does she kneel
  In the twilight stilly;
Lily-clad from throat to heel,
  She, my virgin lily?

Soon the wan, the wistful stars,
  Fading, will forsake her;
Elves of light, on beaming bars,
  Whisper then, and wake her.

Let this friendly pebble plead
  At her flowery grating;
If she hear me will she heed?
  Mabel, I am waiting!

Mabel will be deck'd anon,
  Zoned in bride's apparel;
Happy zone!—oh hark to yon
  Passion-shaken carol!

Sing thy song, thou trancèd thrush,
  Pipe thy best, thy clearest;—
Hush, her lattice moves, oh hush—
  Dearest Mabel!—dearest . . .
      FREDERICK LOCKER-LAMPSON.

CXIII

WHISTLE, AND I'LL COME TO YOU, MY LAD

O WHISTLE, and I'll come to you, my lad;
O whistle, and I'll come to you, my lad;
Tho' father and mither and a' should gae mad,
O whistle, and I'll come to you, my lad.

L

But warily tent, when ye come to court me,
And come na unless the back-yett be a-jee ;
Syne up the back-stile, and let naebody see,
And come as ye were na comin' to me.
O whistle, etc.

At kirk, or at market, whene'er ye meet me,
Gang by me as tho' that ye car'd na a flie :
But steal me a blink o' your bonny black e'e,
Yet look as ye were na lookin' at me.
O whistle, etc.

Aye vow and protest that ye care na for me,
And whiles ye may lightly my beauty a wee ;
But court na anither, tho' jokin ye be,
For fear that she wyle your fancy frae me.
O whistle, etc.

ROBERT BURNS.

CXIV

BELIEVE me, if all those endearing young charms
   Which I gaze on so fondly to-day,
Were to change by to-morrow, and fleet in my arms,
   Like fairy-gifts fading away,
Thou would'st still be adored, as this moment thou art,
   Let thy loveliness fade as it will,
And around the dear ruin each wish of my heart
   Would entwine itself verdantly still.

It is not while beauty and youth are thine own,
   And thy cheeks unprofaned by a tear,
That the fervour and faith of a soul can be known,
   To which time will but make thee more dear ;

No, the heart that has truly loved never forgets,
  But as truly loves on to the close,
As the sun-flower turns on her god, when he sets,
  The same look which she turned when he rose.
                              THOMAS MOORE.

CXV

Ask me no more where Jove bestows,
When June is past, the fading rose;
For in your beauty's orient deep
These flowers, as in their causes, sleep.

Ask me no more, whither do stray
The golden atoms of the day;
For, in pure love, heaven did prepare
Those powers to enrich your hair.

Ask me no more, whither doth haste
The nightingale when May is past;
For in your sweet dividing throat
She winters, and keeps warm her note.

Ask me no more, where those stars light,
That downward fall in dead of night;
For in your eyes they sit, and there
Fixèd become, as in their sphere.

Ask me no more, if east or west,
The phœnix builds her spicy nest;
For unto you at last she flies,
And in your fragrant bosom dies.
                              THOMAS CAREW.

CXVI

Go, lovely rose !
Tell her that wastes her time and me,
That now she knows,
When I resemble her to thee,
How sweet and fair she seems to be.

Tell her that's young,
And shuns to have her graces spy'd,
That hadst thou sprung
In deserts where no men abide,
Thou must have uncommended died.

Small is the worth
Of beauty from the light retired :
Bid her come forth,
Suffer herself to be desired,
And not blush so to be admired.

Then die ! that she
The common fate of all things rare
May read in thee,—　　　.
How small a part of time they share
That are so wondrous sweet and fair.

EDMUND WALLER.

CXVII

DALLYING

DEAR love, I have not ask'd you yet ;
　Nor heard you, murmuring low
As wood-doves by a rivulet,
　Say if it shall be so.

The colour on your cheek which plays,
  Like an imprisoned bliss,
In its unworded language, says,
  "Speak, and I'll answer 'Yes.'"

See, pluck this flower of wood-sorrel,
  And twine it in your hair ;
Its woodland grace becomes you well,
  And makes my rose more fair.

Oft you sit 'mid the daisies here,
  And I lie at your feet ;
Yet day by day goes by ;—I fear
  To break a trance so sweet.

As some first autumn tint looks strange,
  And wakes a strange regret,
Would your soft " yes " our loving change ?—
  Love, I'll not ask you yet.
                                THOMAS ASHE.

CXVIII

PHYLLIS, for shame, let us improve
  A thousand different ways
Those few short moments snatch'd by love
  From many tedious days.

If you want courage to despise
  The censure of the grave,
Though love's a tyrant in your eyes,
  Your heart is but a slave.

My love is full of noble pride,
   Nor can it e'er submit
To let that fop, Discretion, ride
   In triumph over it.

False friends I have, as well as you,
   Who daily counsel me
Fame and ambition to pursue,
   And leave off loving thee.

But when the least regard I show
   To fools who thus advise,
May I be dull enough to grow
   As miserably wise.
     CHARLES SACKVILLE, EARL OF DORSET.

CXIX

TAKE, O take those lips away,
   That so sweetly were forsworn ;
And those eyes, the break of day,
   Lights that do mislead the morn :
But my kisses bring again,
       Bring again,
Seals of love, but sealed in vain,
       Sealed in vain.
     WILLIAM SHAKESPEARE.

CXX

I PRYTHEE send me back my heart,
   Since I can not have thine :
For if from yours you will not part,
   Why then should'st thou have mine ?

Yet now I think on't, let it lie;
  To find it were in vain,
For thou'st a thief in either eye
  Would steal it back again.

Why should two hearts in one breast lie,
  And yet not lodge together?
Oh Love! where is thy sympathy,
  If thus our breasts thou sever?

But love is such a mystery,
  I cannot find it out:
For when I think I'm best resolved,
  I then am in most doubt.

Then farewell care, and farewell woe,
  I will no longer pine;
For I'll believe I have her heart
  As much as she has mine.
                SIR JOHN SUCKLING.

CXXI

KISSING USURY

BIANCHA, let
Me pay the debt
I owe thee for a kiss
  Thou lend'st to me;
  And I to thee
Will render ten for this.

If thou wilt say
Ten will not pay

For that so rich a one,
   I'll clear the sum
   If it will come
Unto a million.

   By this, I guess,
   Of happiness
Who has a little measure,
   He must of right
   To th' utmost mite
Make payment for his pleasure.

          ROBERT HERRICK.

CXXII

CUPID and my Campaspe played
At cards for kisses, Cupid paid ;
He stakes his quiver, bow, and arrows,
His mother's doves, and team of sparrows ;
Loses them too ; then, down he throws
The coral of his lip, the rose
Growing on's cheek (but none knows how)
With these, the crystal of his brow,
And then the dimple of his chin ;
All these did my Campaspe win.
At last he set her both his eyes ;
She won, and Cupid blind did rise.
   O Love ! has she done this to thee ?
   What shall (alas !) become of me ?

          JOHN LYLY.

CXXIII

You that do search for every purling spring
Which from the ribs of old Parnassus flows,
And every flower, not sweet perhaps, which grows
Near thereabouts, into your posy wring ; '
Ye that do dictionary's method bring
Into your rhymes, running in rattling rows ;
You that poor Petrarch's long-deceasèd woes
With new-born sighs and denizen'd wit do sing ;
You take wrong ways ; those far-fetch'd helps be such
As do betray a want of inward touch,
And sure, at length stol'n goods do come to light :
But if, both for your love and skill, your name
You seek to nurse at fullest breasts of Fame,
Stella behold, and then begin to endite.

SIR PHILIP SIDNEY.

CXXIV

THE FAIR SINGER

To make a final conquest of all me,
　Love did compose so sweet an enemy,
In whom both beauties to my death agree,
　Joining themselves in fatal harmony,
That, while she with her eyes my heart does bind,
She with her voice might captivate my mind.

I could have fled from one but singly fair ;
　My disentangled soul itself might save,
Breaking the curlèd trammels of her hair ;
　But how should I avoid to be her slave,
Whose subtle art invisibly can wreathe
My fetters of the very air I breathe ?

It had been easy fighting in some plain,
  Where victory might hang in equal choice ;
But all resistance against her is vain,
  Who has the advantage both of eyes and voice :
And all my forces needs must be undone,
She having gainèd both the wind and sun.

ANDREW MARVELL.

CXXV

LOVE'S IDOLATRY

WHAT you do,
Still betters what is done. When you speak, sweet,
I'd have you do it ever : when you sing,
I'd have you buy and sell so ; so give alms ;
Pray so ; and, for the ordering your affairs,
To sing them too : when you do dance, I wish you
A wave o' the sea, that you might ever do
Nothing but that ; move still, still so, and own
No other function : each your doing,
So singular in each particular,
Crowns what you are doing in the present deed,
That all your acts are queens.

WILLIAM SHAKESPEARE.

CXXVI

THE MANLY HEART

SHALL I, wasting in despair,
Die because a woman's fair?
Or make pale my cheeks with care
'Cause another's rosy are?
Be she fairer than the day
Or the flowery meads in May—
    If she think not well of me
    What care I how fair she be?

Shall my silly heart be pined
'Cause I see a woman kind;
Or a well-disposèd nature
Joinèd with a lovely feature?
Be she meeker, kinder, than
Turtle-dove or pelican,
    If she be not so to me
    What care I how kind she be?

Shall a woman's virtues move
Me to perish for her love?
Or her well-deservings known
Make me quite forget mine own?
Be she with that goodness blest
Which may merit name of Best;
    If she be not such to me,
    What care I how good she be?

'Cause her fortune seems too high
Shall I play the fool and die?
She that bears a noble mind
If not outward helps she find,

Thinks what with them he would do
Who without them dares her woo ;
    And unless that mind I see,
    What care I how great she be ?

Great or good, or kind or fair,
I will ne'er the more despair ;
If she love me, this believe,
I will die ere she shall grieve ;
If she slight me when I woo,
I can scorn and let her go ;
    For if she be not for me,
    What care I for whom she be ?
GEORGE WITHER.

CXXVII

PANSIE

CAME, on a Sabbath noon, my sweet,
    In white, to find her lover.
The grass grew proud beneath her feet,
    The green elm leaves above her—
        Meet we no angels, Pansie ?

She said, " We meet no angels now,"
    And soft lights streamed upon her ;
And with white hand she touched a bough,
    She did it that great honour—
        What, meet no angels, Pansie ?

O sweet brown hat, brown hair, brown eyes,
    Down-dropp'd brown eyes so tender ;
Then what, said I ? gallant replies
    Seem flattery and offend her ;
        But—meet no angels, Pansie ?
THOMAS ASHE.

CXXVIII

I CANNOT change, as others do,
  Though you unjustly scorn,
Since that poor swain that sighs for you,
  For you alone was born ;
No, Phyllis, no, your heart to move
  A surer way I'll try,—
And to revenge my slighted love,
  Will still love on, and die.

When, kill'd with grief, Amintas lies,
  And you to mind shall call
The sighs that now unpitied rise,
  The tears that vainly fall,
That welcome hour that ends his smart
  Will then begin your pain,
For such a faithful tender heart
  Can never break in vain.
        JOHN WILMOT, EARL OF ROCHESTER.

CXXIX

VENUS' RUNAWAY

BEAUTIES, have ye seen this toy,
Called Love, a little boy,
Almost naked, wanton, blind ;
Cruel now, and then as kind ?
If he be amongst ye, say ?
He is Venus' runaway.

He hath marks about him plenty :
You shall know him among twenty.

All his body is a fire,
And his breath a flame entire,
That, being shot like lightning in,
Wounds the heart, but not the skin.

At his sight the sun hath turned,
Neptune in the waters burned ;
Hell hath felt a greater heat ;
Jove himself forsook his seat.
From the centre to the sky
Are his trophies reared high.

Trust him not ; his words, though sweet,
Seldom with his heart do meet.
All his practice is deceit ;
Every gift it is a bait ;
Not a kiss but poison bears ;
And most treason in his tears.

Idle minutes are his reign ;
Then, the straggler makes his gain,
By presenting maids with toys,
And would have ye think them joys :
'Tis the ambition of the elf
To have all childish as himself.

If by these ye please to know him,
Beauties, be not nice, but show him.
Though ye had a will to hide him,
Now, we hope, ye'll not abide him ;
Since you hear his falser play,
And that he's Venus' runaway.

BEN JONSON.

CXXX

IT was a lover and his lass,
  With a hey, and a ho, and a hey nonino,
That o'er the green corn-field did pass
  In the spring time, the only pretty ring time,
When birds do sing, hey ding a ding ding;
Sweet lovers love the spring.

Between the acres of the rye,
  With a hey, and a ho, and a hey nonino,
These pretty country folks would lie.
  In spring time, etc.

This carol they began that hour,
  With a hey, and a ho, and a hey nonino,
How that a life was but a flower
  In spring time, etc.

And therefore take the present time,
  With a hey, and a ho, and a hey nonino,
For love is crowned with the prime
  In spring time, the only pretty ring time,
When birds do sing, hey ding a ding ding;
Sweet lovers love the spring.
                    WILLIAM SHAKESPEARE.

CXXXI

GAZE not upon the stars, fond sage,
  In them no influence lies;
To read the fate of youth or age,
  Look on my Helen's eyes.

Yet, rash astrologer, refrain ;
  Too dearly would be won
The prescience of another's pain,
  If purchased by thine own.
SIR WALTER SCOTT.

CXXXII

MEDIOCRITY IN LOVE REJECTED

GIVE me more love, or more disdain.
  The torrid or the frozen zone.
Bring equal ease unto my pain ;
  The temperate affords me none.
Either extreme, of love or hate,
Is sweeter than a calm estate.

Give me a storm ; if it be love,
  Like Danæ in that golden shower,
I swim in pleasure ; if it prove
  Disdain, that torrent will devour
My vulture-hopes ; and he's possessed
Of heaven, that's but from hell released.
Then drown my joys, or cure my pain ;
Give me more love, or more disdain.
THOMAS CAREW.

CXXXIII

ON A GIRDLE

THAT which her slender waist confined
Shall now my joyful temples bind :
No monarch but would give his crown
His arms might do what this has done.

It was my heaven's extremest sphere,
The pale which held that lovely deer
My joy, my grief, my hope, my love
Did all within this circle move.

A narrow compass ! and yet there
Dwelt all that's good and all that's fair ;
Give me but what this riband bound—
Take all the rest the sun goes round.

EDMUND WALLER.

CXXXIV

TO CELIA

DRINK to me only with thine eyes,
    And I will pledge with mine ;
Or leave a kiss but in the cup,
    And I'll not look for wine.
The thirst that from the soul doth rise
    Doth ask a drink divine :
But might I of Jove's nectar sup,
    I would not change for thine.

I sent thee late a rosy wreath,
    Not so much honouring thee,
As giving it a hope, that there
    It could not withered be.
But thou thereon didst only breathe,
    And sent'st it back to me :
Since when it grows, and smells, I swear,
    Not of itself, but thee.

BEN JONSON.

CXXXV

My love she's but a lassie yet,
A lichtsome lovely lassie yet;
　　It scarce wad do
　　To sit an' woo
Down by the stream sae glassy yet.
But there's a braw time coming yet;
When we may gang a-roaming yet;
　　An' hint wi' glee
　　O' joys to be,
When fa's the modest gloaming yet.

She's neither proud nor saucy yet;
She's neither plump nor gaucy yet;
　　But just a jinking,
　　Bonny blinking,
Hilty-skilty lassie yet.
But O her artless smile's mair sweet
Than hinny or than marmalete;
　　An' right or wrang,
　　Ere it be lang,
I'll bring her to a parley yet.

I'm jealous o' what blesses her,
The very breeze that kisses her,
　　The flowery beds
　　On which she treads,
Though wae for ane that misses her.
Then O to meet my lassie yet,
Up in yon glen sae grassy yet;
　　For all I see
　　Are nought to me
Save her that's but a lassie yet!

　　　　　　　　　　JAMES HOGG.

CXXXVI

ACCEPT, my love, as true a heart
  As ever lover gave :
'Tis free, it vows, from any art,
  And proud to be your slave.

Then take it kindly, as 'twas meant,
  ˙And let the giver live,
Who, with it, would the world have sent,
  Had it been his to give.

And, that Dorinda may not fear
  I e'er will prove untrue,
My vow shall, ending with the year,
  With it begin anew.
                    MATTHEW PRIOR.

CXXXVII

WHO is Silvia? what is she,
  That all our swains commend her?
Holy, fair, and wise is she ;
  The heaven such grace did lend her,
That she might admired be.

Is she kind as she is fair?
  For beauty lives with kindness :
Love doth to her eyes repair,
  To help him of his blindness ;
And, being help'd, inhabits there.

Then to Silvia let us sing,
  That Silvia is excelling ;
She excels each mortal thing
  Upon the dull earth dwelling :
To her let us garlands bring.
                    WILLIAM SHAKESPEARE.

CXXXVIII

SONG

LADIES, though to your conquering eyes
Love owes his chiefest victories,
And borrows those bright arms from you
With which he does the world subdue,
Yet you yourselves are not above
The empire nor the griefs of love.

Then rack not lovers with disdain,
Lest love on you revenge their pain :
You are not free because you're fair,
The boy did not his mother spare :
Though beauty be a killing dart,
It is no armour for the heart.

SIR GEORGE ETHERAGE.

CXXXIX

HONEST lover whosoever,
If in all thy love there ever
Was one wav'ring thought, if thy flame
Were not still even, still the same ;
Know this,
Thou lov'st amiss,
And to love true
Thou must begin again, and love anew.

If, when she appears i' th' room,
Thou dost not quake, and art struck dumb,
And in striving this to cover
Dost not speak thy words twice over,

      Know this,
Thou lov'st amiss,
And to love true
Thou must begin again, and love anew.

If fondly thou dost not mistake,
And all defects for graces take,
Persuad'st thyself that jests are broken
When she has little or nothing spoken,
      Know this,
Thou lov'st amiss,
And to love true
Thou must begin again, and love anew.

If, when thou appear'st to be within,
Thou let'st not men ask and ask again ;
And when thou answer'st, if it be
To what was ask'd thee properly,
      Know this,
Thou lov'st amiss,
And to love true
Thou must begin again, and love anew.

If, when thy stomach calls to eat,
Thou cut'st not fingers 'stead of meat,
And with much gazing on her face
Dost not rise hungry from the place,
      Know this,
Thou lov'st amiss,
And to love true
Thou must begin again, and love anew.

If by this thou dost discover
That thou art no perfect lover,
And desiring to love true
Thou dost begin to love anew,

Know this,
Thou lov'st amiss,
And to love true
Thou must begin again, and love anew.
                    SIR JOHN SUCKLING.

CXL

IF music be the food of love, play on ;
Give me excess of it ; that, surfeiting,
The appetite may sicken, and so die.
That strain again ;—it had a dying fall :
O, it o'ercame my ear like the sweet south,
That breathes upon a bank of violets,
Stealing, and giving odour.—Enough ; no more ;
'Tis not so sweet now as it was before.
O spirit of love, how quick and fresh art thou !
That, notwithstanding thy capacity
Receiveth as the sea, nought enters there,
Of what validity and pitch soever,
But falls into abatement and low price,
Even in a minute ! so full of shapes is fancy,
That it alone is high-fantastical.
                    WILLIAM SHAKESPEARE.

CXLI

RESTORE thy tresses to the golden ore,
Yield Cytherea's son those arks of love ;
Bequeath the heavens the stars that I adore,
And to the Orient do thy pearls remove.
Yield thy hand's pride unto the ivory white,
To Arabian odours give thy breathing sweet ;
Restore thy blush unto Aurora bright,
To Thetis give the honour of thy feet.

Let Venus have thy graces her resigned,
And thy sweet voice give back unto the spheres :
But yet restore thy fierce and cruel mind
To Hyrcan tigers and to ruthless bears.
Yield to the marble thy hard heart again ;
So shalt thou cease to plague, and I to pain.

SAMUEL DANIEL.

CXLII

No more, my dear, no more these counsels try ;
O give my passions leave to run their race ;
Let fortune lay on me her worst disgrace ;
Let folk o'ercharged with brain against me cry ;
Let clouds bedim my face, break in mine eye ;
Let me no steps but of lost labour trace ;
Let all the earth with scorn recount my case,—
But do not will me from my love to fly.
I do not envy Aristotle's wit,
Nor do aspire to Cæsar's bleeding fame ;
Nor ought do care though some above me sit ;
Nor hope nor wish another course to frame
But that which once may win thy cruel heart :
Thou art my wit, and thou my virtue art.

SIR PHILIP SIDNEY.

CXLIII

FALSE though she be to me and love,
    I'll ne'er pursue revenge ;
For still the charmer I approve,
    Though I deplore her change.

In hours of bliss we oft have met,
    They could not always last ;
And though the present I regret,
    I'm grateful for the past.

WILLIAM CONGREVE.

CXLIV

Awake, my heart, to be loved, awake, awake!
The darkness silvers away, the morn doth break,
It leaps in the sky: unrisen lustres shake
The o'ertaken moon. Awake, O heart, awake!

She too that loveth awaketh and hopes for thee:
Her eyes already have sped the shades that flee,
Already they watch the path thy feet shall take: .
Awake, O heart, to be loved, awake, awake!

And if thou tarry from her,—if this could be,—
She cometh herself, O heart, to be loved, to thee;
For thee would unashamèd herself forsake:
Awake to be loved, my heart, awake, awake!

Awake, the land is scattered with light, and see,
Uncanopied sleep is flying from field and tree:
And blossoming boughs of April in laughter shake;
Awake, O heart, to be loved, awake, awake!

Lo all things wake and tarry and look for thee:
She looketh and saith, "O sun, now bring him to me.
Come more adored, O adored, for his coming's sake,
And awake my heart to be loved: awake, awake!"

ROBERT BRIDGES.

CXLV

WHAT light is light, if Silvia be not seen?
What joy is joy, if Silvia be not by?
Unless it be to think that she is by,
And feed upon the shadow of perfection.
Except I be by Silvia in the night,
There is no music in the nightingale;
Unless I look on Silvia in the day,
There is no day for me to look upon:
She is my essence; and I leave to be,
If I be not by her fair influence
Fostered, illumined, cherished, kept alive.
                    WILLIAM SHAKESPEARE.

CXLVI

I NEVER drank of Aganippe well,
Nor ever did in shade of Tempe sit,
And Muses scorn with vulgar brains to dwell;
Poor layman I, for sacred rites unfit.
Some do I hear of poets' fury tell,
But, God wot, wot not what they mean by it;
And this I swear by blackest brook of hell,
I am no pick-purse of another's wit.
How falls it then, that with so smooth an ease
My thoughts I speak; and what I speak doth flow
In verse, and that my verse best wits doth please?
Guess we the cause? What, is it this? Fie, no.
Or so? Much less. How then? Sure, thus it is,—
My lips are sweet, inspired with Stella's kiss.
                    SIR PHILIP SIDNEY.

CXLVII

SONG

To thy lover
Dear, discover
That sweet blush of thine that shameth—
When those roses
It discloses—
All the flowers that Nature nameth.

In free air,
Flow thy hair,
That no more Summer's best dresses
Be beholden
For their golden
Locks, to Phœbus' flaming tresses.

O deliver
Love his quiver ;
From thy eyes he shoots his arrows :
Where Apollo
Cannot follow,
Feathered with his mother's sparrows.

RICHARD CRASHAW.

CXLVIII

TO ELECTRA

I DARE not ask a kiss,
   I dare not beg a smile,
Lest having that, or this,
   I might grow proud the while.

No, no, the utmost share
  Of my desire shall be
Only to kiss that air
  That lately kissèd thee.
                    ROBERT HERRICK.

CXLIX

ECHO, daughter of the air,
  Babbling guest of rocks and hills,
Knows the name of my fierce Fair
  And sounds the accents of my ills.
Each thing pities my despair,
  Whilst that she her lover kills.

Whilst that she—O cruel maid !—
  Doth me and my true love despise ;
My life's flourish is decayed,
  That depended on her eyes.
But her will must be obeyed,
  And well he ends, for love who dies.
                    SAMUEL DANIEL.

CL

DIVINE destroyer, pity me no more,
  Or else more pity me.
Give me more love, ah, quickly give me more,
  Or else more cruelty !
    For left thus as I am,
    My heart is ice and flame ;
  And languishing thus, I
  Can neither live nor die !

Your glories are eclipsed, and hid i' th' grave
  Of this indifferency ;
And Cælia, you can neither altars have,
  Nor I, a deity :
    They are aspects divine,
    That still or smile or shine,
  Or, like the offended sky,
  Frown death immediately.
               RICHARD LOVELACE.

CLI

COME, Sleep ! O Sleep, the certain knot of peace,
The baiting-place of wit, the balm of woe,
The poor man's wealth, the prisoner's release,
The indifferent judge between the high and low ;
With shields of proof shield me from out the prease
Of those fierce darts Despair at me doth throw :
O make in me those civil wars to cease ;
I will good tribute pay, if thou do so.
Take thou of me smooth pillows, sweetest bed,
A chamber deaf of noise and blind of light,
A rosy garland and a weary head :
And if these things, as being thine in right,
Move not thy heavy grace, thou shalt in me,
Livelier than elsewhere, Stella's image see.
               SIR PHILIP SIDNEY.

CLII

TO THE VIRGINS, TO MAKE MUCH OF TIME

GATHER ye rosebuds while ye may,
  Old Time is still a-flying :
And this same flower that smiles to-day
  To-morrow will be dying.

The glorious lamp of heaven, the sun,
   The higher he's a-getting,
The sooner will his race be run,
   And nearer he's to setting.

That age is best which is the first,
   When youth and blood are warmer ;
But being spent, the worse, and worst
   Times, still succeed the former.

Then be not coy, but use your time,
   And while ye may, go marry :
For having lost but once your prime,
   You may for ever tarry.
                   ROBERT HERRICK.

CLIII

THE PASSIONATE SHEPHERD TO HIS LOVE

COME live with me and be my love,
And we will all the pleasures prove
That hills and vallies, dales and fields,
Woods or steepy mountain yields.

And we will sit upon the rocks,
Seeing the shepherds feed their flocks
By shallow rivers to whose falls
Melodious birds sing madrigals.

And I will make thee beds of roses
And a thousand fragrant posies,
A cup of flowers and a kirtle
Embroidered all with leaves of myrtle.

A gown made of the finest wool
Which from our pretty lambs we pull ;
Fair-linèd slippers for the cold,
With buckles of the purest gold.

A belt of straw and ivy-buds,
With coral clasps and amber studs ;
And if these pleasures may thee move,
Come live with me, and be my love.

The shepherd-swain shall dance and sing
For thy delight each May-morning ;
If these delights thy mind may move,
Then live with me, and be my love.

CHRISTOPHER MARLOWE.

CLIV

I ASKED my fair, one happy day,
What I should call her in my lay ;
   By what sweet name from Rome or Greece ;
Lalage, Neæra, Chloris,
Sappho, Lesbia, or Doris,
   Arethusa or Lucrece.

" Ah ! " replied my gentle fair,
" Belovèd, what are names but air ?
   Choose thou whatever suits the line ;
Call me Sappho, call me Chloris,
Call me Lalage or Doris,
   Only—only call me thine."

SAMUEL TAYLOR COLERIDGE.

CLV

BECAUSE I oft in dark abstracted guise
Seem most alone in greatest company,
With dearth of words, or answers quite awry,
To them that would make speech of speech arise,
They deem, and of their doom the rumour flies,
That poison foul of bubbling pride doth lie
So in my swelling breast, that only I
Fawn on myself, and others do despise.
Yet pride, I think, doth not my soul possess
(Which looks too oft in his unflattering glass):
But one worse fault, ambition, I confess,
That makes me oft my best friends overpass,
Unseen, unheard, while thought to highest place
Bends all his powers, even unto Stella's grace.

SIR PHILIP SIDNEY.

CLVI

DEAR, why should you command me to my rest,
When now the night doth summon all to sleep?
Methinks this time becometh lovers best ;
Night was ordained together friends to keep :
How happy are all other living things,
Which though the day disjoin by several flight,
The quiet evening yet together brings,
And each returns unto his love at night !
O thou that else so courteous art to all !
Why shouldst thou, night, abuse me only thus,
That every creature to his kind dost call,
And yet 'tis thou dost only sever us?
Well could I wish it would be ever day,
If when night comes, you bid me go away.

MICHAEL DRAYTON.

CLVII

BASSANIO BEFORE PORTIA'S PORTRAIT

WHAT find I here?
Fair Portia's counterfeit?   What demi-god
Hath come so near creation?   Move these eyes?
Or whether, riding on the balls of mine,
Seem they in motion?   Here are severed lips,
Parted with sugar breath; so sweet a bar
Should sunder such sweet friends : here in her hairs
The painter plays the spider, and hath woven
A golden mesh to entrap the hearts of men,
Faster than gnats in cobwebs.   But her eyes,—
How could he see to do them? having made one,
Methinks it should have power to steal both his,
And leave itself unfurnished.   Yet look, how far
The substance of my praise doth wrong this shadow
In underprizing it, so far this shadow
Doth limp behind the substance.

WILLIAM SHAKESPEARE.

CLVIII

LESBIA hath a beaming eye,
  But no one knows for whom it beameth;
Right and left its arrows fly,
  But what they aim at no one dreameth.
Sweeter 'tis to gaze upon
  My Nora's lid that seldom rises;
Few its looks, but every one
  Like unexpected light surprises!

Oh, my Nora Creina, dear !
  My gentle, bashful Nora Creina !
    Beauty lies
    In many eyes,
  But love in yours, my Nora Creina !

Lesbia wears a robe of gold,
  But all so close the nymph hath laced it,
Not a charm of beauty's mould
  Presumes to stay where nature placed it.
Oh ! my Nora's gown for me,
  That floats as wild as mountain breezes,
Leaving every beauty free
  To sink or swell as Heaven pleases !
Yes, my Nora Creina, dear,
  My simple, graceful Nora Creina !
    Nature's dress
    Is loveliness—
  The dress *you* wear, my Nora Creina !

Lesbia hath a wit refined,
  But, when its points are gleaming round us,
Who can tell if they're designed
  To dazzle merely, or to wound us ?
Pillowed on my Nora's heart,
  In safer slumber Love reposes—
Bed of peace ! whose roughest part
  Is but the crumpling of the roses.
Oh, my Nora Creina, dear !
  My mild, my artless Nora Creina !
    Wit, tho' bright,
    Hath no such light
  As warms your eyes, my Nora Creina !
                THOMAS MOORE.

CLIX

OF CORINNA'S SINGING

WHEN to her lute Corinna sings,
Her voice revives the leaden strings,
And doth in highest notes appear
As any challenged echo clear.
But when she doth of mourning speak,
E'en with her sighs the strings do break.

And as her lute doth live and die,
Led by her passions, so must I :
For when of pleasure she doth sing,
My thoughts enjoy a sudden spring ; -
But if she do of sorrow speak,
E'en from my heart the strings do break.

THOMAS CAMPION.

CLX

LOVE'S PERVERSITY

How strange a thing a lover seems
    To animals that do not love !
Lo, where he walks and talks in dreams,
    And flouts us with his lady's glove ;
How foreign is the garb he wears ;
    And how his great devotion mocks
Our poor propriety, and scares
    The undevout with paradox !
His soul, through scorn of worldly care,
    And great extremes of sweet and gall,
And musing much on all that's fair,
    Grows witty and fantastical ;

He sobs his joy and sings his grief,
    And evermore finds such delight
In simple picturing his relief,
    That plaining seems to cure his plight ;
He makes his sorrow, when there's none ;
    His fancy blows both cold and hot ;
Next to the wish that she'll be won,
    His first hope is that she may not ;
He sues, yet deprecates consent ;
    Would she be captured she must fly ;
She looks too happy and content,
    For whose least pleasure he would die :
Oh, cruelty, she cannot care
    For one to whom she's always kind !
He says he's nought, but, oh, despair,
    If he's not Jove to her fond mind !
He's jealous if she pets a dove,
    She must be his with all her soul ;
Yet 'tis a postulate in love
    That part is greater that the whole ;
And all his apprehension's stress,
    When he's with her, regards her hair,
Her hand, a ribbon of her dress,
    As if his life were only there ;
Because she's constant, he will change,
    And kindest glances coldly meet,
And, all the time he seems so strange,
    His soul is fawning at her feet ;
Of smiles and simple heaven grown tired,
    He wickedly provokes her tears,
And when she weeps, as he desired,
    Falls slain with ecstasies of fears ;
He blames her, though she has no fault,
    Except the folly to be his ;
He worships her, the more to exalt

  The profanation of a kiss ;
 Health's his disease ; he's never well
  But when his paleness shames her rose ;
His faith's a rock-built citadel,
  Its sign a flag that each way blows ;
His o'erfed fancy frets and fumes ;
  And Love, in him, is fierce, like Hate,
And ruffles his ambrosial plumes
  Against the bars of time and fate.
       COVENTRY PATMORE.

CLXI

HEAR, ye ladies that despise,
 What the mighty Love has done ;
Fear examples, and be wise :
 Fair Calisto was a nun ;
Leda, sailing on the stream
 To deceive the hopes of man,
Love accounting but a dream,
 Doted on a silver swan ;
Danæ, in a brazen tower,
Where no love was, loved a shower.

Hear, ye ladies that are coy,
 What the mighty Love can do ;
Fear the fierceness of the boy :
 The chaste moon he makes to woo ;
Vesta, kindling holy fires,
 Circled round about with spies,
Never dreaming loose desires,
 Doting at the altar dies :
Ilion, in a short hour, higher
He can build, and once more fire.
       JOHN FLETCHER.

THE WINGS OF EROS

Love, like a bird, hath perched upon a spray
  For thee and me to hearken what he sings.
Contented, he forgets to fly away,—
  But hush ! . . . remind not Eros of his wings.

CLXII

AND wilt thou leave me thus?
Say nay! say nay! for shame,
To save thee from the blame
Of all my grief and grame.
And wilt thou leave me thus?
Say nay! say nay!

And wilt thou leave me thus,
That have loved thee so long
In wealth and woe among:
And is thy heart so strong
As for to leave me thus?
Say nay! say nay!

And wilt thou leave me thus,
That have given thee my heart
Never for to depart
Neither for pain nor smart:
And wilt thou leave me thus?
Say nay! say nay!

And wilt thou leave me thus,
And have no more pity
Of him that loveth thee?
Alas! thy cruelty!
And wilt thou leave me thus?
Say nay! say nay!

SIR THOMAS WYATT.

CLXIII

THE ADIEU

(Song from *Rokeby*)

" A weary lot is thine, fair maid,
　　A weary lot is thine !
To pull the thorn thy brow to braid,
　　And press the rue for wine !
A lightsome eye, a soldier's mien,
　　A feather of the blue,
A doublet of the Lincoln green,—
　　No more of me you knew,
　　　　　　My love !
　　No more of me you knew.

" This morn is merry June, I trow,
　　The rose is budding fain ;
But she shall bloom in winter snow
　　Ere we two meet again."—
He turned his charger as he spake,
　　Upon the river shore,
He gave his bridle reins a shake,
　　Said, " Adieu for evermore,
　　　　　　My love !
　　And adieu for evermore."

Sir Walter Scott.

CLXIV

DISDAIN RETURNED

He that loves a rosy cheek,
　　Or a coral lip admires,
Or from starlike eyes doth seek
　　Fuel to maintain his fires ;

As old Time makes these decay,
So his flames must waste away.

But a smooth and steadfast mind,
   Gentle thoughts and calm desires,
Hearts with equal love combined,
   Kindle never-dying fires.
Where these are not, I despise
Lovely cheeks or lips or eyes.

No tears, Celia, now shall win
   My resolv'd heart to return;
I have search'd thy soul within,
   And find nought but pride and scorn.
I have learn'd thy arts, and now
Can disdain as much as thou.
Some Power, in my revenge, convey
That love to her I cast away.

THOMAS CAREW.

CLXV

LINES

WHEN the lamp is shattered,
The light in the dust lies dead—
   When the cloud is scattered,
   The rainbow's glory is shed.
When the lute is broken,
Sweet tones are remembered not;
   When the lips have spoken,
Loved accents are soon forgot.

   As music and splendour
Survive not the lamp and the lute,
   The heart's echoes render
No song when the spirit is mute :—

No song but sad dirges,
Like the wind through a ruined cell,
    Or the mournful surges
That ring the dead seaman's knell.

When hearts have once mingled
Love first leaves the well-built nest ;
    The weak one is singled
To endure what it once possest.
    O, Love ! who bewailest
The frailty of all things here,
    Why choose you the frailest
For your cradle, your home, and your bier ?

Its passions will rock thee
As the storms rock the ravens on high :
    Bright reason will mock thee,
Like the sun from a wintry sky.
    From thy nest every rafter
Will rot, and thine eagle home
    Leave thee naked to laughter,
When leaves fall and cold winds come.
                    PERCY BYSSHE SHELLEY.

CLXVI

A LOST OPPORTUNITY

WE might, if you had willed, have conquered heaven.
Only once in our lives before the gate
Of Paradise we stood, one fortunate even,
And gazed in sudden rapture through the grate.
And, while you stood astonished, I, our fate
Venturing, pushed the latch and found it free.
There stood the tree of knowledge fair and great
Beside the tree of life.   One instant we

Stood in that happy garden, guardianless.
My hands already turned towards the tree,
And in another moment we had known
The taste of joy and immortality
And been ourselves as gods.   But in distress
You thrust me back with supplicating arms
And eyes of terror, till the impatient sun
Had time to set and till the heavenly host
Rushed forth on us with clarions and alarms
And cast us out for ever, blind and lost.
                    WILFRID SCAWEN BLUNT.

CLXVII

INGRATEFUL BEAUTY THREATENED

KNOW, Celia, since thou art so proud,
   'Twas I that gave thee thy renown :
Thou hadst, in the forgotten crowd
   Of common beauties, lived unknown,
Had not my verse exhaled thy name,
And with it impt the wings of Fame.

That killing power is none of thine,
   I give it to thy voice and eyes :
Thy sweets, thy graces, all are mine ;
   Thou art my star, shin'st in my skies ;
Then dart not from thy borrowed sphere
Lightning on him that fix'd thee there.

Tempt me with such affrights no more,
   Lest what I made I uncreate :
Let fools thy mystic forms adore,
   I'll know thee in thy mortal state.
Wise poets, that wrapt truth in tales,
Knew her themselves through all her veils.
                    THOMAS CAREW.

CLXVIII

THE SCRUTINY

WHY should'st thou swear I am forsworn,
    Since thine I vowed to be?
Lady, it is already morn,
    And 'twas last night I swore to thee
    That fond impossibility.

Have I not loved thee much and long,
    A tedious twelve hours' space?
I must all other beauties wrong,
    And rob thee of a new embrace,
    Could I still dote upon thy face.

Not but all joy in thy brown hair
    By others may be found ;
But I must search the black and fair,
    Like skilful mineralists that sound
    For treasures in unploughed-up ground.

Then if, when I have loved my round,
    Thou prov'st the pleasant she,
With spoils of meaner beauties crowned
    I laden will return to thee,
    Ev'n sated with variety.
                      RICHARD LOVELACE.

CLXIX

FALSE LOVE

(THE GLOVE AND THE LIONS)

KING Francis was a hearty king, and loved a royal
    sport,
And one day as his lions fought sat looking on the court;

The nobles filled the benches, with the ladies in their
 pride,
And 'mongst them sat the Count de Lorge, with one for
 whom he sighed :
And truly 'twas a gallant thing to see that crowning
 show,
Valour and love, and a king above, and the royal beasts
 below.

Ramp'd and roar'd the lions, with horrid laughing jaws ;
They bit, they glared, gave blows like beams, a wind
 went with their paws ;
With wallowing might and stifled roar they rolled on one
 another,
Till all the pit with sand and mane was in a thunderous
 smother ;
The bloody foam above the bars came whisking through
 the air ;
Said Francis then, " Faith, gentlemen, we're better here
 than there."

De Lorge's love o'erheard the king, a beauteous lively
 dame
With smiling lips and sharp bright eyes, which always
 seem'd the same :
She thought, the Count my lover is brave as brave can
 be ;
He surely would do wondrous things to show his love of
 me ;
King, ladies, lovers, all look on; the occasion is divine ;
I'll drop my glove to prove his love; great glory will be
 mine.

She dropp'd her glove, to prove his love, then look'd at
 him and smiled ;
He bowed, and in a moment leapt among the lions wild :

The leap was quick, return was quick, he has regain'd
    his place,
Then threw the glove, but not with love, right in the
    lady's face.
"By Heaven!" said Francis, "rightly done!" and he
    rose from where he sat :
"No love," quoth he, "but vanity, sets love a task like
    that."

LEIGH HUNT.

CLXX

ON A WOMAN'S INCONSTANCY

I LOVED thee once, I'll love no more ;
Thine be the grief as is the blame ;
Thou art not what thou wast before,
What reason I should be the same ?
He that can love, unloved again,
Hath better store of love than brain :
God send me love my debts to pay,
While unthrifts fool their love away.

Nothing could have my love o'erthrown
If thou hadst still continued mine ;
Yea, if thou hadst remained thy own,
I might perchance have still been thine.
But thou thy freedom didst recall,
That it thou might'st elsewhere enthrall ;
And then how could I but disdain,
A captive's captive to remain ?

When new desires had conquered thee,
And changed the object of thy will,
It had been lethargy in me,
No constancy, to love thee still.

Yea, it had been a sin to go
And prostitute affection so,
Since we are taught no prayers to say
To such as must to others pray.

Yet do thou glory in thy choice,
Thy choice of his good fortune boast ;
I'll neither grieve nor yet rejoice,
To see him gain what I have lost.
The height of my disdain shall be
To laugh at him, to blush for thee ;
To love thee still, but go no more
A-begging at a beggar's door.

SIR ROBERT AYTON.

CLXXI

SONG OF GLYCINE

A SUNNY shaft did I behold,
   From sky to earth it slanted :
And poised therein a bird so bold—
   Sweet bird, thou wert enchanted !
He sank, he rose, he twinkled, he trolled
   Within that shaft of sunny mist ;
His eyes of fire, his beak of gold,
   All else of amethyst !

And thus he sang : " Adieu ! adieu !
Love's dreams prove seldom true.
The blossoms they make no delay :
The sparkling dew-drops will not stay.
   Sweet month of May,
      We must away :
      Far, far away !
         To-day ! to-day !"

SAMUEL TAYLOR COLERIDGE.

CLXXII

THE GUEST

LIGHTS Love, the timorous bird, to dwell,
　　While summer smiles, a guest with you?
Be wise betimes and use him well,
　　And he will stay in winter too:
For you can have no sweeter thing
Within the heart's warm nest to sing.

The blue-plumed swallows fly away,
　　Ere autumn gilds a leaf; and then
Have wit to find, another day,
　　The little clay-built house again:
He will not know, a second spring,
His last year's nest, if Love take wing.
THOMAS ASHE.

CLXXIII

SEPARATION

STOP!—not to me, at this bitter departing,
　　Speak of the sure consolations of time!
Fresh be the wound, still-renew'd be its smarting,
　　So but thy image endure in its prime.

But, if the steadfast commandment of Nature
　　Wills that remembrance should always decay—
If the loved form and the deep-cherish'd feature
　　Must, when unseen, from the soul fade away—

Me let no half-effaced memories cumber!
　　Fled, fled at once be all vestige of thee!
Deep be the darkness and still be the slumber—
　　Dead be the past and its phantoms to me!

Then, when we meet, and thy look strays towards me,
  Scanning my face and the changes wrought there :
Who, let me say, *is this stranger regards me,*
  With the gray eyes, and the lovely brown hair?
                              MATTHEW ARNOLD.

CLXXIV

TO MY INCONSTANT MISTRESS

WHEN thou, poor excommunicate
  From all the joys of love, shalt see
The full reward and glorious fate
  Which my strong faith shall purchase me,
  Then curse thine own inconstancy.

A fairer hand than thine shall cure
  That heart which thy false oaths did wound ;
And to my soul, a soul more pure
  Than thine shall by love's hand be bound,
  And both with equal glory crown'd.

Then shalt thou weep, entreat, complain
  To Love, as I did once to thee ;
When all thy tears shall be as vain
  As mine were then, for thou shalt be
  Damned for thy false apostacy.
                              THOMAS CAREW.

CLXXV

SINCE there's no help, come let us kiss and part.
Nay, I have done, you get no more of me,
And I am glad, yea, glad with all my heart,
That thus so cleanly I myself can free.
Shake hands for ever, cancel all our vows,
And when we meet at any time again,
Be it not seen in either of our brows
That we one jot of former love retain.

Now at the last gasp of love's latest breath,
When his pulse failing, passion speechless lies,
When faith is kneeling by his bed of death,
And innocence is closing up his eyes,
Now if thou wouldst, when all have given him over,
From death to life thou might'st him yet recover.

MICHAEL DRAYTON.

CLXXVI
A FAREWELL

WITH all my will, but much against my heart,
We two now part.
My very Dear,
Our solace is, the sad road lies so clear.
It needs no art,
With faint, averted feet
And many a tear,
In our opposed paths to persevere.
Go thou to East, I West.
We will not say
There's any hope, it is so far away.
But, O, my Best,
When the one darling of our widowhead,
The nursling Grief,
Is dead,
And no dews blur our eyes
To see the peach-bloom come in evening skies,
Perchance we may,
Where now this night is day,
And even through faith of still averted feet,
Making full circle of our banishment,
Amazed meet ;
The bitter journey to the bourn so sweet
Seasoning the termless feast of our content
With tears of recognition never dry.

COVENTRY PATMORE.

LOVE WITH MANY LYRES

He strikes a hundred lyres, a thousand strings,
Yet one at heart are all the songs he sings.

SHE was a phantom of delight
When first she gleam'd upon my sight ;
A lovely Apparition, sent
To be a moment's ornament ;
Her eyes as stars of twilight fair ;
Like Twilight's, too, her dusky hair ;
But all things else about her drawn
From May-time and the cheerful dawn ;
A dancing shape, an image gay,
To haunt, to startle, and waylay.

I saw her upon nearer view,
A Spirit, yet a Woman too !
Her household motions light and free,
And steps of virgin-liberty ;
A countenance in which did meet
Sweet records, promises as sweet ;
A creature not too bright or good
For human nature's daily food,
For transient sorrows, simple wiles,
Praise, blame, love, kisses, tears, and smiles.

And now I see with eye serene
The very pulse of the machine ;
A being breathing thoughtful breath,
A traveller between life and death :

The reason firm, the temperate will,
Endurance, foresight, strength, and skill;
A perfect Woman, nobly plann'd,
To warn, to comfort, and command;
And yet a Spirit still, and bright
With something of an angel-light.

WILLIAM WORDSWORTH.

CLXXVIII

SONG

WHEN I am dead, my dearest,
　Sing no sad songs for me;
Plant thou no roses at my head,
　Nor shady cypress tree:
Be the green grass above me
　With showers and dewdrops wet;
And if thou wilt, remember,
　And if thou wilt, forget.

I shall not see the shadows,
　I shall not feel the rain;
I shall not hear the nightingale
　Sing on, as if in pain:
And dreaming through the twilight
　That doth not rise nor set,
Haply I may remember,
　And haply may forget.

CHRISTINA GEORGINA ROSSETTI.

CLXXIX

SHE is not fair to outward view,
　As many maidens be ;
Her loveliness I never knew
　Until she smiled on me.
O then I saw her eye was bright,
A well of love, a spring of light.

But now her looks are coy and cold,
　To mine they ne'er reply,
And yet I cease not to behold
　The love-light in her eye :
Her very frowns are fairer far
Than smiles of other maidens are.
HARTLEY COLERIDGE.

CLXXX

MY letters ! all dead paper, mute and white !
And yet they seem alive and quivering
Against my tremulous hands which loose the string
And let them drop down on my knee to-night.
This said,—he wished to have me in his sight
Once, as a friend : this fixed a day in spring
To come and touch my hand . . . a simple thing,
Yet I wept for it !—this . . . the paper's light . . .
Said, *Dear, I love thee* ; and I sank and quailed
As if God's future thundered on my past.
This said, *I am thine*—and so its ink has paled
With lying at my heart that beat too fast.
And this . . . O Love, thy words have ill availed
If, what this said, I dared repeat at last !
ELIZABETH BARRETT BROWNING.

CLXXXI

THERE grew a lowly flower by Eden-gate
Among the thorns and thistles. High the palm
Branched o'er her, and imperial by her side
Upstood the sunburnt Lily of the east.

The goodly gate swung oft with many gods
Going and coming, and the spice-winds blew
Music and murmurings, and paradise
Welled over and enriched the outer wild.

Then the palm trembled fast-bound by the feet,
And the imperial Lily bowed her down
With yearning, but they could not enter in.

The lowly flower she looked up to the palm
And lily, and at eve was full of dews,
And hung her head and wept and said, "Ah these
Are tall and fair, and shall I enter in?"

There came an angel to the gate at even,
A weary angel, with dishevelled hair;
The blossoms of his crown fell one by one
Through many nights, and seemed a falling star.

He saw the lowly flower by Eden-gate;
And cried, "Ah, pure and beautiful!" and turned
And stooped to her and wound her in his hair,
And in his golden hair she entered in.

Husband! I was the weed at Eden-gate;
I looked up to the lily and the palm
Above me, and I wept and said, "Ah these
Are tall and fair, and shall I enter in?"
And one came by me to the gate at even,
And stooped to me and wound me in his hair,
And in his golden hair I entered in.

SYDNEY DOBELL.

CLXXXII

LOVESIGHT

WHEN do I see thee most, beloved one?
   When in the light the spirits of mine eyes
   Before thy face, their altar, solemnise
The worship of that Love through thee made known?
Or when in the dusk hours (we two alone)
   Close-kissed and eloquent of still replies
   Thy twilight-hidden glimmering visage lies,
And my soul only sees thy soul its own?

O love, my love! if I no more should see
Thyself, nor on the earth the shadow of thee,
   Nor image of thine eyes in any spring,—
How then should sound upon life's darkening slope
The ground-whirl of the perished leaves of Hope,
   The wind of Death's imperishable wing?

                         DANTE GABRIEL ROSSETTI.

CLXXXIII

TRUST me, I have not earned your dear rebuke;
   I love, as you would have me, God the most;
   Would lose not Him, but you, must one be lost,
Nor with Lot's wife cast back a faithless look
Unready to forego what I forsook;
   This say I, having counted up the cost,
   This, though I be the feeblest of God's host,
The sorriest sheep Christ shepherds with his crook.
Yet while I love my God the most, I deem
   That I can never love you overmuch;

I love Him more, so let me love you too ;
Yea, as I apprehend it, love is such
I cannot love you if I love not Him,
  I cannot love Him if I love not you.
     CHRISTINA GEORGINA ROSSETTI.

CLXXXIV

IF thou must love me, let it be for nought
Except for love's sake only.　Do not say
" I love her for her smile—her look—her way
Of speaking gently,—for a trick of thought
That falls in well with mine, and certes brought
A sense of pleasant ease on such a day "—
For these things in themselves, Belovèd, may
Be changed, or change for thee,—and love, so wrought
May be unwrought so.　Neither love me for
Thine own dear pity's wiping my cheek dry,—
A creature might forget to weep, who bore
Thy comfort long, and lose thy love thereby !
But love me for love's sake, that evermore
Thou mayst love on, through love's eternity.
     ELIZABETH BARRETT BROWNING.

CLXXXV

ANY POET TO HIS LOVE

IMMORTAL Verse !　Is mine the strain
To last and live?　As ages wane
What hand for me will twine the bays?
Who'll praise me then as now you praise?

Will there be one to praise?　Ah no !
My laurel leaf may never grow ;
My bust is in the quarry yet,
Oblivion weaves my coronet.

Immortal for a month—a week !
The garlands wither as I speak ;
The song will die, the harp's unstrung,
But, singing, have I vainly sung ?

You deign'd to lend an ear the while
I trill'd my lay.   I won your smile.
Now, let it die, or let it live,—
My verse was all I had to give.

The linnet flies on wistful wings,
And finds a Bower, and lights and sings ;
Enough if my poor verse endures
To light and live—to die in Yours.
                    FREDERICK LOCKER-LAMPSON.

CLXXXVI

I WISH I could remember that first day,
    First hour, first moment of your meeting me,
    If bright or dim the season, it might be
Summer or Winter for aught I can say ;
So unrecorded did it slip away,
    So blind was I to see and to foresee,
    So dull to mark the budding of my tree
That would not blossom yet for many a May.
If only I could recollect it, such
    A day of days !   I let it come and go
    As traceless as a thaw of bygone snow ;
It seemed to mean so little, meant so much ;
If only now I could recall that touch,
    First touch of hand in hand—Did one but know !
                    CHRISTINA GEORGINA ROSSETTI.

CLXXXVII

LOGAN BRAES

By Logan's streams that rin sae deep
Fu' aft, wi' glee, I've herded sheep,
I've herded sheep, or gather'd slaes,
Wi' my dear lad, on Logan braes.
But wae's my heart ! thae days are gane
And fu' o' grief I herd alane,
While my dear lad maun face his faes,
Far, far frae me and Logan braes.

Nae mair, at Logan Kirk, will he,
Atween the preachings, meet wi' me—
Meet wi' me, or when it's mirk,
Convoy me hame frae Logan kirk.
.I weel may sing thae days are gane—
Frae kirk and fair I come alane
While my dear lad maun face his faes
Far, far frae me and Logan braes.

At e'en, when hope amaist is gane,
I dander dowie and forlane,
Or sit beneath the trysting-tree,
Where first he spak' of love to me.
O ! could I see thae days again,
My lover skaithless, and my ain,
Rever'd by friends, and far frae faes,
We'd live in bliss on Logan braes.

John Mayne.

CLXXXVIII

THOUGH I am young and cannot tell
Either what Death or Love is well,
Yet I have heard they both bear darts,
And both do aim at human hearts :
And then again, I have been told
Love wounds with heat, as Death with cold ;
So that I fear they do but bring
Extremes to touch, and mean one thing.

As in a ruin we it call
One thing to be blown up, or fall ;
Or to our end like way may have
By flash of lightning, or a wave :
So love's inflamed shaft or brand
May kill as soon as Death's cold hand,
Except Love's fires the virtue have
To fright the frost out of the grave.

BEN JONSON.

CLXXXIX

ONE YEAR AGO

ONE year ago my path was green,
My footstep light, my brow serene ;
Alas ! and could it have been so
   One year ago ?
There is a love that is to last
When the hot days of youth are past :
Such love did a sweet maid bestow
   One year ago.
I took a leaflet from her braid
And gave it to another maid.
Love ! broken should have been thy bow
   One year ago.

WALTER SAVAGE LANDOR.

CXC

On the way to Kew,
By the river old and gray,
Where in the Long Ago
We laughed and loitered so,
I met a ghost to-day,
A ghost that told of you,
A ghost of low replies
And sweet inscrutable eyes,
    Coming up from Richmond,
As you used to do.

By the river old and gray,
The enchanted Long Ago
Murmured and smiled anew.
On the way to Kew,
March had the laugh of May,
The bare boughs looked aglow,
And old immortal words
Sang in my breast like birds,
    Coming up from Richmond,
As I used with you.

With the life of Long Ago
Lived my thought of you.
By the river old and gray
Flowing his appointed way,
As I watched, I knew
What is so good to know :
Not in vain, not in vain,
I shall look for you again,
    Coming up from Richmond,
On the way to Kew.
                WILLIAM ERNEST HENLEY.

CXCI

How do I love thee?   Let me count the ways.
I love thee to the depth and breadth and height
My soul can reach, when feeling out of sight
For the ends of Being and ideal grace.
I love thee to the level of every day's
Most quiet need, by sun and candlelight.
I love thee freely, as men strive for Right ;
I love thee purely, as they turn from praise.
I love thee with the passion put to use
In my old griefs, and with my childhood's faith.
I love thee with a love I seemed to lose
With my lost saints,—I love thee with the breath,
Smiles, tears, of all my life !—and, if God choose,
I shall but love thee better after death.

ELIZABETH BARRETT BROWNING.

CXCII

THREE KISSES OF FAREWELL

THREE, only three, my darling,
  Separate, solemn, slow ;
Not like the swift and joyous ones
  We used to know,
When we kissed because we loved each other,
  Simply to taste love's sweet,
And lavished our kisses as the summer
  Lavishes heat ;
But as they kiss whose hearts are wrung,
  When hope and fear are spent,
And nothing is left to give, except
  A sacrament !

First of the three, my darling,
　　Is sacred unto pain ;
We have hurt each other often,
　　We shall again,
When we pine because we miss each other,
　　And do not understand
How the written words are so much colder
　　Than eye and hand.
I kiss thee, dear, for all such pain
　　Which we may give or take ;
Buried, forgiven before it comes,
　　For our love's sake.

The second kiss, my darling,
　　Is full of joy's sweet thrill ;
We have blessed each other always,
　　We always will.
We shall reach until we feel each other
　　Beyond all time and space :
We shall listen till we hear each other
　　In every place ;
The earth is full of messengers,
　　Which love sends to and fro ;—
I kiss thee, darling, for all joy
　　Which we shall know !

The last kiss, oh ! my darling—
　　My love—I cannot see,
Through my tears, as I remember
　　What it may be.
We may die and never see each other,
　　Die with no time to give
Any signs that our hearts are faithful
　　To die, as live.

Token of what they will not see
    Who see our parting breath,
This one last kiss, my darling,
    The seal of death !
AGNES E. GLASE.

CXCIII

AWAY, delights ; go seek some other dwelling,
    For I must die.
Farewell, false love ; thy tongue is ever telling
    Lie after lie :
For ever let me rest now from thy smarts ;
    Alas, for pity, go
    And fire their hearts
That have been hard to thee !   Mine was not so.

Never again deluding love shall know me,
    For I will die ;
And all those griefs that think to over-grow me
    Shall be as I :
For ever will I sleep, while poor maids cry,
    " Alas, for pity, stay,
    And let us die
With thee !   Men cannot mock us in the clay."
JOHN FLETCHER.

CXCIV

I NEVER gave a lock of hair away
To a man, Dearest, except this to thee,
Which now upon my fingers thoughtfully
I ring out to the full brown length, and say,
" Take it."   My day of youth went yesterday ;
My hair no longer bounds to my foot's glee,
Nor plant I it from rose or myrtle-tree

P

As girls do, any more ; it only may
Now shade on two pale cheeks the mark of tears,
Taught drooping from the head that hangs aside
Through sorrow's trick.   I thought the funeral-shears
Would take this first, but love is justified,—
Take it thou,—finding pure, from all those years,
The kiss my mother left here when she died.

ELIZABETH BARRETT BROWNING.

CXCV

THOU didst delight my eyes :
Yet who am I ? nor first
Nor last nor best, that durst
Once dream of thee for prize ;
Nor this the only time
Thou shalt set love to rhyme.

Thou didst delight my ear :
Ah ! little praise ; thy voice
Makes other hearts rejoice,
Makes all ears glad that hear ;
And short my joy ; but yet,
O song, do not forget.

For what wert thou to me ?
How shall I say ? the moon,
That poured her midnight noon
Upon his wrecking sea ;—
A sail, that for a day
Has cheered the castaway.

ROBERT BRIDGES.

CXCVI

GENIUS IN BEAUTY

BEAUTY like hers is genius.   Not the call
  Of Homer's or of Dante's heart sublime,—
  Not Michael's hand furrowing the zones of time,—
Is more with compassed mysteries musical ;
Nay, not in Spring's or Summer's sweet footfall
  More gathered gifts exuberant Life bequeaths
  Than doth this sovereign face, whose love-spell
    breathes
Even from its shadowed contour on the wall.

As many men are poets in their youth,
  But for one sweet-strung soul the wires prolong
  Even through all change the indomitable song ;
So in likewise the envenomed years, whose tooth
Rends shallower grace with ruin void of ruth,
  Upon this beauty's power shall wreck no wrong.
                    DANTE GABRIEL ROSSETTI.

CXCVII

FAUSTUS TO THE APPARITION OF HELEN

  WAS this the face that launched a thousand ships
  And burnt the topless towers of Ilium ?
  Sweet Helen, make me immortal with a kiss.
  Her lips suck forth my soul ; see where it flies !—
  Come, Helen, come, give me my soul again.
  Here will I dwell, for heaven is in these lips,
  And all is dross that is not Helena.
  I will be Paris, and for love of thee,
  Instead of Troy, shall Wertenberg be sacked :

And I will combat with weak Menelaus,
And wear thy colours on my plumèd crest :
Yea, I will wound Achilles in the heel,
And then return to Helen for a kiss.
Oh, thou art fairer. than the evening air
Clad in the beauty of a thousand stars ;
Brighter art thou than flaming Jupiter
When he appeared to hapless Semele :
More lovely than the monarch of the sky
In wanton Arethusa's azured arms ;
And none but thou shall be my paramour.

CHRISTOPHER MARLOWE.

CXCVIII

My Damon was the first to wake
    The gentle flame that cannot die ;
My Damon is the last to take
    The faithful bosom's softest sigh :
The life between is nothing worth,
    Oh, cast it from thy thought away ;
Think of the day that gave it birth,
    And this its sweet returning day.

Buried be all that has been done,
    Or say that naught is done amiss ;
For who the dangerous path can shun
    In such bewildering world as this ?
But love can every fault forgive,
    Or with a tender look reprove ;
And now let naught in memory live,
    But that we meet, and that we love.

GEORGE CRABBE.

CXCIX

JEANIE MORRISON

I'VE wandered east, I've wandered west,
　　Through many a weary way;
But never, never can forget
　　The luve o' life's young day!
The fire that's blawn on Beltane e'en,
　　May weel be black 'gin yule;
But blacker fa' awaits the heart
　　Where first fond luve grows cule.

O dear, dear Jeanie Morrison,
　　The thochts o' bygone years
Still fling their shadows ower my path,
　　And blind my e'en wi' tears:
They blind my e'en wi' saut, saut tears,
　　And sair and sick I pine,
As memory idly summons up
　　The blythe blinks o' langsyne.

'Twas then we luvit ilk ither weel,
　　'Twas then we twa did part;
Sweet time—sad time! twa bairns at scule,
　　'Twa bairns, and but ae heart!
'Twas then we sat on ae laigh bink,
　　To leir ilk ither lear;
And tones and looks and smiles were shed,
　　Remembered evermair.

I wonder, Jeanie, aften yet,
　　When sitting on that bink,
Cheek touchin' cheek, loof lock'd in loof,
　　What our wee heads could think?

When baith bent doun ower ae braid page,
　　Wi' ae buik on our knee,
Thy lips were on thy lesson, but
　　My lesson was in thee.

Oh, mind ye how we hung our heads,
　　How cheeks brent red wi' shame,
Whene'er the scule-weans laughin' said,
　　We cleek'd thegither hame?
And mind ye o' the Saturdays
　　(The scule then skailt at noon),
When we ran aff to speel the braes—
　　The broomy braes o' June?

My head rins round and round about,
　　My heart flows like a sea,
As ane by ane the thochts rush back
　　O' scule-time and o' thee.
O mornin' life! O mornin' luve!
　　O lichtsome days and lang,
When hinnied hopes around our hearts
　　Like simmer blossoms sprang!

Oh mind ye, luve, how aft we left
　　The deavin' dinsome toun,
To wander by the green burnside,
　　And hear its waters croon?
The simmer leaves hung ower our heads,
　　The flowers burst round our feet,
And in the gloamin' o' the wood
　　The throssil whusslit sweet;—

The throssil whusslit in the wood,
　　The burn sang to the trees,
And we, with Nature's heart in tune,
　　Concerted harmonies;

And on the knowe abune the burn,
  For hours thegither sat
In the silentness o' joy, till baith
  Wi' very gladness grat.

Aye, aye, dear Jeanie Morrison,
  Tears trinkled doun your cheek,
Like dew-beads on a rose, yet nane
  Had ony power to speak !
That was a time, a blessed time,
  When hearts were fresh and young,
When freely gushed all feelings forth,
  Unsyllabled, unsung !

I marvel, Jeanie Morrison,
  Gin I hae been to thee,
As closely twined wi' earliest thochts
  As ye hae been to me ?
Oh, tell me gin their music fills
  Thine ear as it does mine ;
Oh, say gin e'er your heart grows grit
  Wi' dreamings o' langsyne ?

I've wandered east, I've wandered west,
  I've borne a weary lot ;
But in my wanderings far or near
  Ye never were forgot.
The fount that first burst frae this heart
  Still travels on its way ;
And channels deeper as it rins,
  The luve o' life's young day.

O dear, dear Jeanie Morrison,
  Since we have sindered young,
I've never seen your face, nor heard
  The music o' your tongue ;

But I could hug all wretchedness,
  And happy could I dee,
Did I but ken your heart still dreamed
  · O' bygane days and me !
                    WILLIAM MOTHERWELL.

CC

IF there be any one can take my place
  And make you happy whom I grieve to grieve,
  Think not that I can grudge it, but believe
I do commend you to that nobler grace,
That readier wit than mine, that sweeter face ;
  Yea, since your riches make me rich, conceive
  I too am crowned, while bridal crowns I weave,
And thread the bridal dance with jocund pace.
For if I did not love you, it might be
  That I should grudge you some one dear delight ;
    But since the heart is yours that was mine own,
  Your pleasure is my pleasure, right my right,
Your honourable freedom makes me free,
    And you companioned I am not alone.
                    CHRISTINA G. ROSSETTI.

CCI

LOVE'S FATALITY

SWEET LOVE,—but oh ! most dread Desire of Love,
  Life-thwarted.   Linked in gyves I saw them stand,
  Love shackled with Vain-longing, hand in hand :
And one was eyed as the blue vault above :
But hope tempestuous like a fire-cloud hove
  I' the other's gaze, even as in his whose wand
  Vainly all night with spell-wrought power has spann'd
The unyielding caves of some deep treasure-trove.

Also his lips, two writhen flakes of flame,
    Made moan : " Alas O Love, thus leashed with me !
    Wing-footed thou, wing-shouldered, once born free :
And I, thy cowering self, in chains grown tame,—
Bound to thy body and soul, named with thy name,—
    Life's iron heart, even Love's Fatality."
                DANTE GABRIEL ROSSETTI.

CCII

LOVE'S RETROSPECT

  Lo ! mirror of delight in cloudless days,
Lo ! thy reflection : 'twas when I exclaimed,
With kisses hurried as if each foresaw
Their end, and reckon'd on our broken bonds,
And could at such a price such loss endure,
" O what to faithful lovers met at morn,
What half so pleasant as imparted fears ?"
Looking recumbent how Love's column rose
Marmoreal, trophied round with golden hair,
How in the valley of one lip unseen
He slumber'd, one his unstrung bow impressed.
Sweet wilderness of soul-entangling charms !
Led back by Memory, and each blissful maze
Retracing, me with magic power detain
Those dimpled cheeks, those temples violet-tinged,
Those lips of nectar and those eyes of heaven !
              WALTER SAVAGE LANDOR.

CCIII

IF I freely may discover
What would please me in my lover,
I would have her fair and witty,
Savouring more of court than city;
A little proud, but full of pity:
Light and humorous in her toying,
Oft building hopes, and soon destroying,
Long, but sweet in the enjoying;
Neither too easy nor too hard:
All extremes I would have barred.

BEN JONSON.

CCIV

AH, Chloris! could I now but sit
    As unconcerned as when
Your infant beauty could beget
    No happiness or pain!
When I the dawn used to admire,
    And praised the coming day,
I little thought the rising fire
    Would take my rest away.

Your charms in harmless childhood lay
    Like metals in a mine;
Age from no face takes more away
    Than youth conceal'd in thine.
But as your charms insensibly
    To their perfection press'd,
So love as unperceived did fly,
    And centred in my breast.

My passion with your beauty grew,
  While Cupid at my heart,
Still as his mother favoured you,
  Threw a more flaming dart :
Each gloried in their wanton part ;
  To make a lover, he
Employ'd the utmost of his art—
  To make a beauty, she.

SIR CHARLES SEDLEY.

CCV

LOVE AND LAUGHTER

IN the days when Earth was young,
  Love and Laughter roamed together :
Love took up her harp and sung,
  Round him all was golden weather,
But there came a sigh anon—
What will be when Life is done ?

Laughter then would try his skill,
  Sang of mirth and joy undying :
But he played his part so ill,
  He set Echo all a-sighing.
Ever came an undertone—
What will be when Life is done ?

Then for ever since that time,
  Love no more can live with Laughter ;
For bright as is the summer's prime,
  Winter pale will follow after.
Love henceforth must dwell with sighs :
Joy was left in Paradise.

ARTHUR GREY BUTLER.

CCVI

I WILL not let thee go.
Ends all our month-long love in this?
    Can it be summed up so,
    Quit in a single kiss?
    I will not let thee go.

I will not let thee go.
If thy words' breath could scare thy deeds,
    As the soft south can blow
    And toss the feathered seeds,
    Then might I let thee go.

I will not let thee go.
Had not the great sun seen, I might;
    Or were he reckoned slow
    To bring the false to light,
    Then might I let thee go.

I will not let thee go.
The stars that crowd the summer skies
    Have watched us so below
    With all their million eyes,
    I dare not let thee go.

I will not let thee go.
Have we not chid the changeful moon,
    Now rising late, and now
    Because she set too soon,
    And shall I let thee go?

I will not let thee go.
Have not the young flowers been content,
    Plucked ere their buds could blow,
    To seal our sacrament?
    I cannot let thee go.

I will not let thee go.
I hold thee by too many bands :
   Thou sayest farewell, and lo !
   I have thee by the hands,
   And will not let thee go.

ROBERT BRIDGES.

NOTES

NOTES

I. *Midsummer Night's Dream*, Act I. Scene i.

V. Fitz-Eustace's Song, in *Marmion*.

IX. No less accomplished a critic than Mr. Palgrave would appear to prefer the following version :—

> Ye flowery banks o' bonny Doon,
>   How can ye bloom sae fair !
> How can ye chant, ye little birds,
>   And I sae fu' o' care !
>
> Thou'lt break my heart, thou bonny bird,
>   That sings upon the bough ;
> Thou mind'st me o' the happy days
>   When my fause luve was true.
>
> Thou'lt break my heart, thou bonny bird,
>   That sings beside thy mate ;
> For sae I sat, and sae I sang,
>   And wist na o' my fate.
>
> Aft hae I roved by bonny Doon,
>   To see the woodbine twine,
> And ilka bird sang o' its luve,
>   And sae did I o' mine.
>
> Wi' lichtsome heart I pu'd a rose,
>   Frae off its thorny tree ;
> And my fause luver staw the rose,
>   But left the thorn wi' me.

XI. Campbell has treated the same subject, but much more unsatisfactorily, in his song beginning—

> "Earl March looks on his dying child."

XIII. From *Eloisa to Abelard*.

Q

XIV. Written on board the ship which conveyed Keats to Italy. There is another version in which the last line reads as follows :—

"And so live ever, or else swoon to death "—

a reading adopted by Mr. Forman and Mr. W. M. Rossetti, but which seems to me less beautiful.

XVI. From *Harold*; a Drama.

XVIII. From *The Human Tragedy*.

XIX. From *The Corsair*, being the second and third stanzas of a song containing four.

XXIV. From *Horton*, a narrative poem in blank verse.

XXV. *All's Well that Ends Well*, Act I. Scene i.

XXVIII. From *Eloisa to Abelard*. The line,

"Obedient slumbers that can wake and weep,"

is taken bodily from Crashaw, and does not seem to me an instance of very felicitous borrowing—the somewhat fantastic manner (albeit founded upon the classical usage of transferring a quality from a person to a thing) being scarcely in harmony with Pope's own more direct and simple style.

XXXIII. From *Epipsychidion*.

XXXVI. The first stanza is ancient, the rest Scott's.

XXXVIII. Lady Heron's Song, in *Marmion*.

XLI. The version embodying its author's own emendations is adopted.

XLIII. From *Don Juan*, Canto ii.

XLIV. The version given by Lord Houghton is adopted here. Mr. Forman prefers the following variant, which seems to me, wherever it differs from the other, to differ for the worse :—

Ah, what can ail thee, wretched wight,
    Alone and palely loitering?
The sedge is withered from the lake,
    And no birds sing.

Ah, what can ail thee, wretched wight,
    So haggard and so woe-begone?
The squirrel's granary is full,
    And the harvest's done.

I see a lily on thy brow,
  With anguish moist and fever-dew ;
And on thy cheek a fading rose
  Fast withereth too.

I met a lady in the meads,
  Full beautiful, a faery's child ;
Her hair was long, her foot was light,
  And her eyes were wild.

I set her on my pacing steed,
  And nothing else saw all day long ;
For sideways would she lean, and sing
  A faery's song.

I made a garland for her head,
  And bracelets too, and fragrant zone ;
She look'd at me as she did love,
  And made sweet moan.

She found me roots of relish sweet,
  And honey wild, and manna dew ;
And sure in language strange she said,
  " I love thee true."

She took me to her elfin grot,
  And there she gazed and sighed deep,
And there I shut her wild sad eyes
  So kiss'd to sleep.

And there we slumber'd on the moss,
  And there I dream'd, ah woe betide,
The latest dream I ever dream'd
  On the cold hill side.

I saw pale kings, and princes too,
  Pale warriors, death-pale were they all ;
Who cried—" La Belle Dame sans merci
  Hath thee in thrall ! "

I saw their starved lips in the gloam
  With horrid warning gapèd wide,
And I awoke and found me here
  On the cold hill side.

And this is why I sojourn here
  Alone and palely loitering,
Though the sedge is withered from the lake,
  And no birds sing.

XLVI. From *An Hymne in Honour of Beautie.*

XLIX. From *Festus.*   Compare the opening lines—

  " I loved her for that she was beautiful ;
    And that to me she seemed to be all nature,
    And all varieties of things in one :"

with Rossetti—

> "Sometimes thou seem'st not as thyself alone,
> But as the meaning of all things that are."

L. From *Love's Widowhood*, Stanzas lxix. and lxx.

LIII. From *Childe Harold's Pilgrimage*, Canto iii.

LIV. I omit two stanzas.

LV. *Midsummer Night's Dream*, Act I. Scene i.

LVI. From *The Curse of Kehama*.

LVIII. From *The Angel in the House*.

LIX. *Fairy Queen*, Book VI. Canto xi. Stanza i.

LX. From the Eighth Book of *Paradise Lost*.

LXI. From *An Hymne in Honour of Love*.

LXIV. From *The Devil is an Ass*. This is the second stanza of a song having two. The piece is clumsily imitated by Suckling.

LXXI. From *Amours de Voyage*.

LXXIII. Stanza ii. line 6 ; *stare = starling*.

LXXIV. Two prelusive stanzas omitted as excrescent and superfluous.

LXXX. From *The Haunted Glen*. Two versions exist, and the one here given is an amalgam of both.

LXXXI. *Cymbeline*, Act. II. Scene iii.

LXXXV. This is sometimes printed "When the kye *come* hame." Hogg himself resented strongly this tampering with a familiar Scottish phrase for the sake of syntax.

XC. *Childe Harold's Pilgrimage*, Canto iii.

XCI. From *The Two Noble Kinsmen*. Mr. Swinburne confidently assumes Shakespeare's part in the authorship of the play to have included this beautiful song. Mr. A. H. Bullen gives it "tentatively to Fletcher," but adds, " I have a strong suspicion that it is by Shakespeare." I have adopted the emendations of Seward and other modern editors, the version in the older editions being obviously corrupt.

XCII. Line 7—
> "The gods that wanton in the air."

Mr. W. C. Hazlitt adheres to "birds" instead of "gods," in accordance with the MS. printed by the late Dr. Bliss, in his edition of Wood's *Athenæ*. I see no reason, however, for departing from the earliest printed text, which reads *gods*.

Line 10. "Alloying" would really come nearer to conveying Lovelace's obvious meaning than "allaying," as implying the admixture of a baser element, which "allaying" scarcely does.

XCIII. *Fairy Queen*, introduction to Book IV. Stanza ii.

CIII. *Fairy Queen*, Book III. Canto v. Stanza i.

CIV. Stanza iii. lines 3, 4—
> "Could make divine affection cheap,
> And court his golden birth,"

i.e. "could make divine affection cheap, and *make it* court his golden birth."

CVIII. In this fine piece there is yet, to my thinking, somewhat too much of a despotic or autocratic tone. One thinks of Spenser's lines—

> "Ne may Love be compelled by maisterie :
> For soon as maisterie comes, sweete Love anon
> Taketh his nimble wings, and soon away is gone."

CX. From *Romeo and Juliet*, Act II. Scene ii.

CXIX. From *Measure for Measure*. The late Mr. Halliwell-Phillips was "inclined to think" that this song is not Shakespeare's.

CXXI. Referring to the last stanza, Dr. Grosart says : "By Hazlitt and others the commencement is put first in this stanza." I follow "Hazlitt and others," for the sufficient reason (as it seems to me) that the stanza is, in the form they adopt, intelligible, and in the other arrangement absolutely meaningless.

CXXII. Song of Apelles in *Campaspe*.

CXXIII. In this sonnet I have ventured to substitute "betray" for "bewray," and "far-fetch'd" for "far-fet."

CXXV. *Winter's Tale,* Act IV. Scene iii.

CXXX. From *As You Like It.* In the first line of the refrain "ring time" is Stevens's emendation of "rank time."

CXXXI. Quoted (?) by Scott, in *A Legend of Montrose,* as "marked with the quaint hyperbolical taste of King Charles's time."

CXXXIII. The apparently defective rhymes, so frequent in our elder poets, are doubtless in many cases due to a pronunciation which has perished, or is only perpetuated in provincial dialects. Had "crown" and "done" been pronounced in Waller's time as in our own, it is inconceivable that he could have yoked them as in this lyric.

CXXXVII. From *Two Gentlemen of Verona,* Act IV. Scene ii.

CXXXVIII. From *Love in a Tub.*

CXXXIX. Stanza i. line 3. This would scan, which it does not at present, if transposed thus—

> " If in all thy love there ever
> *One wav'ring thought was, if thy flame,*" etc.

I rather think this was what Suckling wrote, or meant to write.

CXL. *Twelfth Night,* Act I. Scene i. In the penultimate line "fancy" is used to mean "love"—as in "Tell me, where is fancy bred," and "In maiden meditation fancy-free."

CXLI. Query—In last line, should "pain" be "plain"?

CXLV. *Two Gentlemen of Verona,* Act III. Scene i.

CXLVII. These are the first three stanzas of a piece containing seven, which its author calls *Song, out of the Italian.* Cp. last line—

> " Feathered with his mother's sparrows,"

with Jonson—

> " He hath plucked her doves and sparrows
> To feather his sharp arrows."

CXLIX. These are the third and last stanzas of an ode having four.

CLII. Compare Spenser—

> Gather, therefore, the rose while yet is prime,
> For soon comes age, that will his pride deflower :
> Gather the rose of love while yet is time."

CLVII. *Merchant of Venice*, Act III. Scene ii.

CLX. From *The Angel in the House.*

CLXI. From *Valentinian*, by Beaumont and Fletcher.

CLXII. To tamper with the text of Wyatt does certainly appear audacious ; yet, as nothing is lost in point of sense or sound, while much is gained in the matter of syntax, by the alteration, I have been so temerarious as to substitute " have " for " hath " in the second line of the second and third stanzas of this beautiful poem.

CLXIII. From *The Pirate.*

CLXVII. Modern anthologists have mostly printed the beautiful concluding couplet as follows :—

> " Wise poets who wrap truth in tales
> Knew her themselves through all her veils,"

thus disregarding the awkward confusion of tenses which their error produces, and suggesting the suspicion that a corrupt source has been relied upon for the text.   I do not know that the error occurs in any editions of Carew antecedent to Chalmers's flagrantly inaccurate one.   The correct reading is obviously that in the original edition, 1640.

CLXVIII. In the earliest editions the first line reads, " Why *should you* swear I am forsworn," but " should'st thou " agrees so much better with the " thine " of the line that follows, etc., that I have ventured to adopt it, being further fortified by the known fact that no text of Lovelace can be regarded as quite immaculate.

CLXX. Stanza ii. line 8—

> " A captive's captive to remain."

Compare Shakespeare—

> " But slave to slavery my sweet'st friend must be."

CLXXXI. One of the songs of Amy in that vast, amorphous production *Balder* ; a work of which the prevalent gloom is relieved by passages of great sweetness, and others of extravagant splendour.

CLXXXVIII. From *The Sad Shepherd*.

CXCIII. From *The Captain*, by Beaumont and Fletcher.

CXCVII. From *The Tragicall Historie of Dr. Faustus*.

CCII. From *Gebir*, Book IV.

CCIII. From *The Poetaster*.

CCVI. Written, evidently, in conscious and direct imitation of Wyatt. See Wyatt's two lyrics given in this volume.

INDEX OF FIRST LINES

THE END

Printed by R. & R. CLARK, *Edinburgh*

www.ingramcontent.com/pod-product-compliance
Lightning Source LLC
Chambersburg PA
CBHW031401020726
47499CB00005B/1468